THRU THE PROJECT WINDOW

NANCY M BOWLING

ISBN: 979-8-89075-870-5

CONTENTS

Chapter 1: Rough Beginning

In the beginning, there was love, there was peace, there was harmony in its most dysfunctional way, but it worked. I wouldn't say that life was a pretty picture or a glamorous television show, but we made the best of what we had until the bomb went off in the inner city. This bomb would have a larger impact than heroin.

Being the eldest child of a dysfunctional family, I had to grow up fast. I had my childhood stolen and was put into a position of forced adulthood, taking care of others and ensuring that those I loved were as safe as possible. As I've become an actual adult, I have learned that my need to care for others was partially born out of necessity, an internal need to provide nurture. I grew up fast, like so many other children of color in the early 80s and 90s, to parents who fell victim to drug addiction, with me having both my parents and stepparents falling prey to the ravages of crack, putting the responsibilities of parenting them myself and my siblings on my tiny shoulders, most of these responsibilities I've carried into adulthood.

The black community was at war with itself, starting in our own households. Family wasn't family anymore; aunts, uncles, cousins, neighbors, grandparents, and parents fell into this vicious cycle of searching for the next high. Children in this time know all too well the heartache, embarrassment, pain, and suffering inflicted on the black community and all communities of color in the 80s and 90s. We know about food stamps welfare lines, boiling water on stove tops to take a bath, lighting candles because the power was turned off due to lack of payment, and standing on the food pantry lines because the refrigerator and cabinets are bare. Sleeping fully clothed because there is no heat, washing clothes in the sink or tub until your knuckles are red, sore, and raw, or having BCW knocking on your door and removing you from your home. Do you know how it feels to be the only kid at the book fair with no money? Do you know how it is to be on a school trip watching your peers eat huge subs, and you open your bag to see a boiled egg, so you pretend you didn't have anything to eat at all? We weren't born with silver or gold spoons in our mouths. We were born having to fight directly into a struggle. Many of us flourished; however, a lot of us have failed, and some stubbled along the way, traveling through hellfire. I'm one who stumbled along the way, making bad decisions and walking a trail of fire lined with many errors, tears, and triumphs. Being the eldest child, I've endured a lot of pain and heartache, and honestly, it has made me a fucking amazing person. I wish I could say I had the luxury to be a naïve, gullible, unexperienced child, but I can't.

I tell everyone I've been working since the age of eight because that's when my life got flipped upside down and turned inside out. From the age of eight, I became a provider. This is when Nurse Monique was born. This was my alter ego when I had to transform from a child to the strong backbone of my family unit, living and growing up in turmoil. Now, it wasn't an instant change. My parents kind of maintained and held their own for a little while, but the call of the pipe was just too strong.

Growing up, one should never have to pray that you are born into a strong family that possesses morals and values and would teach you right from wrong. That should be the norm. Unfortunately, it's not the norm. It's damn near a foreign concept. I was created out of young love and the fact that my parents didn't have a safe place to call home. They would become each other's safe place. Wherever they were together would become home. My mother let us call her Amber, and my father let us call him Kevin. They were from the same projects (Eagle Edge) located in Canton, New Brunswick. My parents were quite young when they had me. My mother, a short thick, and shapely young lady with an ass like a pony the color of

8

coffee with cream, turned 18 in March of '79, and my father, a tall thin athletic build chocolate man with an afro that could have rivaled Michael Jacksons turned 18 in December, '79. I made my entrance into this shit hole of a world in October '79. I'm their first and only child together, and even though my parents were young, they tried to stay together and be a family; however, a certain situation (my grandmother, Lynn) kept them apart, which led to them finding love and opportunities elsewhere. I'm the eldest of seven children. My parents separated when I turned two. They had tried their hardest to make it work; however, their age and my grandma Lynn made it hard for them to stay together and be a family. When my mother had me, she had been staying out in Wakefield with her mother, my grandma, Sunny. Tuesday, October 2nd, Amber was walking the boardwalk on a bright afternoon, eating a Nathan's hotdog with mustard and onions, and drinking an orange ice cream soda when I decided to present myself to the world at 11:02 pm under an Aquarius full moon high tide. I have no idea what any of this means, but my mother told me this bit of information, so I guess it's important. We lived out in Wakefield with Sunny and her mother, my great-grandmother, Joannie, until I was about two years old. My father made weekly trips out there and would stay for about two to four days before going back to Eagle Edge. He would eventually grow tired of this and ask his mother, Lynn, if Amber and I could move in. She would agree and then renege on her word, and we would end up with James.

Something that I find wildly funny is my earliest memory is not of my parents or a loving family member. No, it is of the man who would soon father three of my siblings, the man who would be a part of a horrible portion of my childhood once introduced to crack. This memory is of the very first meeting. Let us call him James. James, the color of caramel with a big head, was a little more muscular than my father but shorter, and he was older than both my mother and father. James worked a few odd and end jobs but lived off of his disability check he got while working in a factory, and some machine fucked his arm up. We were in the park across the street from where my father and grandmother Lynn lived. This man had French fries drenched in ketchup, salt, pepper, and hot sauce. My mother introduced me to James, and he offered me a fry. I ate them all. Damn shame my stomach has always been the way to my heart. Tickle my fancy with food, and you could kidnap me. I mean, once the food is gone, you would want to return me; however, in the interim, I will become your best friend. My mother and I had been staying with my aunt Crystal and her first baby daddy, Bruce Lee. After that meeting in the park, we went to live with James at his grandmother's apartment in Pleasantville. She was a sweet old lady with dementia. I really don't remember much about her other than we had to get a special lock put on the door because she would leave at night, and the police would bring her back home after being picked up from wandering the streets. My mother had sewed the address onto her nightgowns and robes and spoke with her daughter Anne often. Amber became like her home health aide, so we had a free ride and lived pretty comfortably with what Anne paid Amber and what James brought home.

I want to talk about my mother here for a second and shed some light on her upbringing. I don't want you to think that she is a heartless monster, the likes of "Joan Crawford Mommie Dearest." She provided us with the best she could. She didn't live a nice, cozy life filled with rainbows and kittens. Her mother left her and her siblings when she was around ten, and the man who was supposed to care for her was an abusive, alcoholic, pedophilic madman. She was never shown love or how to give love properly. Amber stored all her hurt, pains, and joys deep down within her so no one could or would ever find them. She would become a living and breathing shell, almost like a puppet controlled by men used and taken advantage of. And on top of that she now had to become a mother to her siblings at the age of ten. While she should have been a normal adolescent, she couldn't; she was forced into becoming an adult way too early in life. Eerily similar to the path of mother and daughter.

Now, at this point in my story, we are going to put a small pin on my father's side, not that my father and his side of the family didn't play a huge part in my life. The earlier years were mainly spent with my mother and James. And from the age of two and a half to eight, life was pretty normal. A twist on the Norman Rockwell Thanksgiving painting is that we would become a blended family. My sister Joy was born in '84, a beautiful little girl with a ton of hair on her head and rose-colored cheeks, looking as if someone had pinched her when she exited the womb. For the first 2-3 years after Joy's birth, I had no complaints until one of my mother's younger sisters, let us call her Rose, introduced my mother and James to Crack Cocaine. Rose was my grandmother, Sunnie's third child. She could have been a Mariah Carey impersonator and she had men fawning all over her.

Rose had the looks and the attitude to boot. She, like my mother, had a rough upbringing; however, she never let the world know it was wearing her down, so she moved like she was royalty and demanded respect from everyone she encountered. It didn't matter what she did for a living. What mattered was that she was a person, and all people deserve to be respected until they aren't. Now, I will admit their usage was more recreational at first. In fact, their drug use was not even noticeable. We still went camping, learned how to fish and start fires, roast marshmallows over an open flame, had a refrigerator full of food, and all the bills paid; life was decent. I'll even admit that James was a cool stepdad. He taught me how to ride my bike without training wheels, how to fish, and how to crab. Amber taught me how to gut the fish, clean them, and start a fire. You see, my mother and James are kind of wilderness nuts, so camping and survival in the woods were a thing, so should there ever be a zombie apocalypse, I'll survive thanks to them. However, the descent was a slow spiral into what one must consider hell on earth. That Norman Rockwell picture soon melted into a living nightmare in Pleasantville. We went from eating every night to praying for tea and toast or being thankful for school lunch. We never had money; however, it didn't become apparent to me until I would ask for simple things like toilet tissue, milk, and food, and the response was I'll see what I can do. Which usually meant begging, borrowing, or stealing. Let's not talk about clothing and shoes. That's a joke. Highwaters and holey hand-me-downs would become life.

Being in school meant that I would have at least two meals for that day: breakfast and lunch. Being in school, I also learned that the more fortunate kids were the cool kids, and those kids would be mean, cold, and cruel to the misfortunate. We would become the butt of their jokes and the gum on the bottom of their new Nikes. I went from being the pretty little girl with long hair to the kids on my block making fun of me for what I would say was petty and irrelevant childish things like me no longer bringing lunch but eating school lunch or having holes in my clothes mismatched socks however, as a child those things leave a thin layer of scars on you, and you either toughen up or get steamrolled over. From this point on, I started to build my armor, developing a thick skin and having a not giving a fuck kind of attitude which I would need because I would become a surrogate mother for my siblings and parents, and I would need to be tough to endure what was to come. I would start to morph into this nesting mom who needed to make sure everyone, and I mean everyone, was okay, safe, and secure. I had no time to mop around and feel sorry for myself or let people's words cause me stress. A tremendous amount of pressure to be placed on an eight-year-old. But I held it together through neglect, assault, and abandonment. I would hold my head up as highly as possible and bury all my needs and wants away, as I learned from Amber and Rose.

While in the second grade, my mother developed a safety word for me to use should a stranger approach me. You know, stranger danger was a popular term back in the 80s. Sometimes, my mother would let me walk to and from school by myself. She gave me a code word. The thought was that this word would prevent me from getting snatched off the streets. Yes, a code word was a magical protector. And in all honesty, the code just let me know that my mother had sent someone for me so I wouldn't be afraid to go with them, and so, my word was 'Bug-a-boo.' Yes, when that song with the same name dropped many years later, I laughed to myself. Now, my 'Bug-a-boo' was the name of an elf doll I had gotten as a birthday gift from one of the neighbors. He was dressed in green, white, and red, of course, Christmas colors. He was an elf. However, what made me love this little doll was his eyes and the facial expression that had been painted onto his face. He had a soft brown-colored face, and he was a little older with a little smirk like he had just heard a funny joke or story. 'Bug-a-boo' looked like he had just become a grandfather; he just gave off love and affection. Yes, I got all this from his face. Perhaps I made it up because I lacked this in my life, but it's the feeling I received from him; I had another doll. Well, he's more of a stuffed animal. His name is Humphrey. Humphrey was given to me at birth by Sunny, my grandmother. He has been through a lot, and I still have him as an adult. He holds a special place in my heart, for he has been my personal diary since I could speak. The stories that stuffed animals could tell if he could speak would have you clutching your pearls.

As life in Pleasantville spun out of control, the apartment that we lived in would turn into a crack den at night and occasionally spilled over into the morning. My mother tried to shield us, Joy and I, from it, but I was very aware that my pretty normal life was not pretty or normal anymore. Oh, I failed to mention James is also from the same project as my parents, so he had friends who still lived in that area. One night, James and my mother loaded us up in the car that James's father gave him as a birthday gift, and we drove to Canton to visit one of his friends. Let us call him Oscar. Oscar was a frail-looking older man the color of a butterscotch candy. He lived in what was once called the square. We entered his apartment, and there were quite a few people already there, none of whom I knew besides Oscar.

As we walked into the crowded apartment there was a foul odor and smoke in the air. Dark figures that I knew were people crowded into the living room and kitchen. In the living room, in the far corner, was a tattered black loveseat with a corner table. The table held a homemade-looking lamp with a red light bulb, which was the only source of light in the front. James made his way over to Oscar. They kept Joy upfront with them since she was asleep in her stroller. My mom took my dungaree jacket and ushered me into the back with Oscar's two sons, and yes, you can tell what happened already from the setup. However, for me, at the fresh age of eight, going on nine, it's a devastating, traumatic, life-altering experience, and the weirdest thing is that I'm so grateful that it only happened to me once.

What a thing to be thankful for. I, unlike so many other little black girls and boys who got assaulted repeatedly, suffered through it once, and it changed me forever. I can't imagine repeated offenses. I don't know if I'd been strong enough to live through such damming experiences multiple times. Well, his sons said, "Hello, Miss Amber," and she said hello and asked us to behave, and she walked back to the front. Oscar's younger son closed the door once my mother was out of sight, turned off the light, and said we're gonna play a game; he was about fifteen. Now, the only light in the room was coming from the window.

I was confused, and before I could say anything, Oscar's older son threw me onto the bed. He was about eighteen, maybe nineteen. The younger son held me down while his older son pulled my pants and

14

panties down and whispered to me, "I'm gonna make you a woman today." I struggled to get free, but then the older son punched me so hard that all the air rushed from my lungs. Now frozen in fear, I couldn't scream. I couldn't move; I couldn't do anything but lay there and then, what felt like a hot scorching pain that ripped through my body as he entered my frail, undeveloped, untouched lower private area with no mercy pounding into me like he was trying to break me in half I started to scream at that point, but he placed his hand over my mouth. What was left of my innocence was being stolen. My eyes began to burn with tears. My head was spinning because I didn't know what was happening to me, but I knew it was wrong. I don't know how long this torture went on. I just stared out of that project window, praying for God to rescue me and save me from this horror. As I lay there praying, my mind ran to my sister, feverishly praying my sister was okay in the front. If I was being tortured, I prayed for her protection and that she wouldn't be next. I don't know how long he had been inside and on top of me when I suddenly felt his body jerk, and then the weight of his entire body dropped down on me, and hands that once held me down now threw a shirt at me and said, "Wipe off. It's my turn." The older brother, still on top of me, whispered to me, "Now you're a woman, and this is how a man shows his love."

When he rolled over and off me, he told his younger brother to leave me alone and that I'd had enough. Just let her be. He had already started to pull his pants down. He obeyed but had a rebuttal, saying something like he never lets him have any fun, and at that point, I lost myself and track of the time. I don't remember putting my clothes on, leaving or getting in the car, and going home. I don't remember getting in the bed that Joy and I shared. In fact, I really don't recall the next few days after that. I can vaguely remember my mother asking me what was wrong. I guess I was walking around like a zombie or something, and so I said nothing. I wanted to protect her feelings. I didn't want her to know she had failed me. Her feelings meant more to me than my own. She was strong and fragile, all at once a rose with thorns dangled over a vat of acid, as I imagine her. Amber couldn't save herself. How was she supposed to save me? It was at this point I started having an unhealthy relationship with my mother and the expectations I had of her. At this point, the expectations I had of her no longer existed, and I began to treat her as a guardian and not a parent. Eventually, she would become my guardian in name only because she was older than me, roles would reverse, and I would become the parent. This would be the new norm in the household.

A few years later, I would overhear James and my mother talking, and they said that Oscar died of walking pneumonia. I would learn that shortly after his passing, his oldest son would OD (overdose)and die. I have no clue what happened to his youngest son, not that it matters, but I kind of hope he got run over by a Mack Truck. I know I shouldn't have such disdain for one of God's children; however, if you ask me, they are the spawn of the devil sent here to steal the joy and light from young girls, and they deserve to suffer. The other part of me forgives them because they were children as well, much older than I was, but children nonetheless. But hey, I ain't perfect, nor am I God, so fuck them and the whole the crawled out of. Please give me some grace. God is still working on me, and through me, it's a process.

The words and actions of the older brother would become seared and imprinted onto my soul. A scar would form that would not heal or wash away a memory, a tiny voice that would creep up on me and invade my thoughts and dreams. Those actions, those words that violate my body, trust, and youth, would make me feel unloved, unprotected, forgotten, unwanted, undervalued, not appreciated, alone, lonely, not worthy, and all the other unkind and unfriendly words, thoughts and feelings one can feel or think about themselves. This self-loathing and self-hate would now become a part of me, of how I viewed myself for what seems most of my life here on earth. I kept the sexual assault to myself and didn't tell anyone what had happened to me for years. I was too ashamed of what had transpired, feeling like it was my fault. That I, as a child, had allowed this horrible act to happen to me. How could I just lie there and not fight back? This must be some kind of punishment that I deserved. I would play mind games with myself, saying that the assault and any and everything harmful or hurtful that happened to me was deserved because I let someone down. These were the warped thoughts that circulated in my head and would hold on tight like a chilled wind ushering in the fall. These feelings and thoughts would sometimes consume me and terrorize me for years. But God is a good God, and with prayer and therapy, I'm a work in progress. And being honest with myself and loving myself, I'm stronger than I've ever been.

CHAPTER 2: UNINTENTIONAL NEGLECT

A few months after the sexual assault occurred, life in the apartment in Pleasantville got worse. Our electricity got cut off, and my mother had to ask James's mother for some help to get the power restored. Around this time, James had started frequently abusing my mother and forcing her to prostitute. He'd make her sell herself to buy drugs and then beat her for having sex. Try to make that make sense. Anyway, at a young age, I didn't know why there were so many men coming and going. Still, it was all to fuel James's growing addiction, and with the in-and-out traffic increasing in the apartment, Joy and I were mainly secluded in the bedroom we shared. My only solace was either when my father picked me up for the weekend or when I was in school. On one Saturday morning, after a night of holding Joy and keeping her calm because of the fighting and my mom screaming and hearing her being beaten and thrown around, I guess my mother had enough and decided she was going to leave this world and Joy and I behind. Joy asked if I would walk her to the bathroom, and I placed her small, slender hand into my own slender hand and exited the bedroom. We walked in on our mother, drinking a bottle of rubbing alcohol. This was the first attempt I would see. Upon seeing this action, it didn't make me feel sad that she wanted to leave because her life was horrible. Instead, it enraged me. How could the person who was supposed to care for and protect me just want to leave me and Joy to fend for ourselves? This only enforced those feelings of a lonely little girl on a night when her innocence was taken away.

On that Saturday, I learned that I had no one to really protect me, no one to look up to. I was to become my own superhero if I was to survive the world that I was living in. On that Saturday, I saw the fragility of my mother. I saw her humanity being stripped away from her. I saw her become broken, and it caused me pain because I couldn't fix her. She was done, couldn't go on anymore, wanted to be free and released from captivity, and needed to escape. I hadn't realized I was screaming, maybe from the shock of seeing Amber ingesting the fluid, or maybe I was having my own breakdown, but the fact was James and I came running into the living room where we all were standing and grabbed what was left of the rubbing alcohol from her hands and mouth. I'm not sure if I called or James called 911 but they were called. The paramedics arrived and took her to the emergency room. She was gone for a few hours and returned as though nothing had happened. No explanation, not a single word. Life just continued to implode around us, bombs being dropped, fires popping up, and us just standing there to see the carnage. About two weeks after that incident, I was walking home from school, and a stranger stepped into my path and tried to stop me. I walk around her and quicken my pace, but then she says Bug a boo. The only person who knows that name is my mother, so she must have sent her. I stopped and turned toward her, looked her up and down, and shook my head. The company my mother and James kept was horrible. This lady had about five rotten teeth left in her mouth, inflamed skin with oozing sores, and a matted red wig. She still had a good weight to her, but she smelled funny, kind of like burnt rubber. She smiled and said, "My girl Amber taught you right cause you weren't playing, honey." She extended her hand and said, "I'm Brook." I just stared at her hand. She had red chipped nail polish with what I assumed was dirt under her nails. She finally took notice of my facial expression and said, "Your parents might not be home yet, so I have the key to let you in," She lowered her hand. I said, "OK," and walked alongside Brook, wondering where my mother and James could be to send this lady to intercept me on my way home. Brook and I came to my building. She used the keys that my mother had given her and asked if I was hungry. I said no, knowing that there more than likely wasn't anything in the apartment to eat. As she opened the door, Joy came running, her face full of life, wonder, and cheer. She always made me smile when I came home from school, the small bit of warmth and sunshine in that damn apartment. Brook said, "Oh, they must be back from the hospital." "Hospital?" Panic floods my body, and I can't move forward. My feet felt glued to the position I was in, scared to walk any further into that apartment to discover what they had to go to the hospital for. Scared to see that I might not find Amber there, my mind started to race about what would happen to Joy and me, and then I heard her voice. My feet were finally able to move from the spot they seemed to have been cemented to. I walked toward my mother's voice to find my mother on crutches and a brace from her ankle to mid-thigh. She never said what happened, but I assumed that it was James or one of the crackheads that frequented my apartment. Not paying attention to the words coming out of her mouth, I was relieved she was there; I still had her presence, and the little protection she provided still provided me with a false sense of security. I hugged her around her waist. She was still taller than me at this point. However, in an instant, I snapped out of my feelings of comfort and relief because I saw Joy out of the corner of my eye and knew I couldn't rely on that false sense of security she provided. I had someone to look out for and make sure she was good. I had to worry about Joy. She was my main priority. Her well-being and her happiness would now be my job. I couldn't allow what happened to me or my mother to be Joy's life. She needed to be sheltered from as much of this world as possible, and she needed to remain pure until she could make her own decisions. Her smiles brought light into my now hardening heart. Every day after school, I would begin the interrogation. I would sit her down and ask her if anyone touched her or put their hands on her body parts. I drilled into her that no one in that house except Amber and I was allowed to touch her, and to my relief, her answer was always no. James had two older sisters, and one would get Joy on a regular basis and have her on the weekends, so I knew she would be safe and taken care of. That alleviated some of the stress and eased a small burden off my shoulders, so a big thank you to Aunt Mirama. Thank you for loving Joy as your own, and thank you for keeping her safe whenever you could. Thank you for introducing her to a happy family setting. She needed that piece of joy in a life full of chaos.

I guess by this point, some of you are feeling sorry for me and wondering how this is even possible. In contrast, others have experienced similar situations growing up and can completely relate. In contrast, some may still feel that I'm lucky because they had it far worse and say hey, at least your parents were not physically abusive to you; however, neglect in any form is abuse, and trust me, I didn't luck out. I have stories about being beaten and tortured, and I will not get that deep here, but I will share one. Before moving to Chicago, I spent the night at my paternal grandmother's apartment, Grandma Lynn. Lynn, the oldest of four children, was a strong, defiant, beautiful, tall single Black mother with thick shoulder-length black hair from the Indian in our family. My grandfather, her first husband, would overdose when my father was nine. Lynn was angry at the world and took her aggression out on everyone. She felt entitled to respect because she laid on her back and pushed out three kids. As she reminds us all the time, "If it were not for me, y'all would not be here." The one thing I will give Lynn is that she taught me to be tough and hard. Never let anyone, no matter who they are, disrespect me or walk over me; she was and is strong like that. I didn't appreciate this about her until I was much older.

Now, on this stay over, one of my younger cousins, Michi, and I decided to play barber shop. Michi is a short, thick, beautiful, brown-skinned girl with a scar under her eye. Michi would cut a huge chunk of hair from the middle of my head. During the game, during which I never got the chance to cut Michi's hair, Kevin walked in on her cutting mine. Not only did Kevin, my father, smack the shit out of me, but when he dropped me back home to my mother Amber, she would beat me with the broom until it broke in half. She beat me with that half until it flew out of her hand, then she beat me with the brush until it cracked, then she beat me with her hands until she tired herself out, and I was limp and bruised. Following this beating, whenever it was time to wash and braid my hair, she would get mad and pop me in my head with the comb multiple times because she could not catch the short hairs on my crown, and this went on until the middle of my hair grew back.

I once told my therapist, yes, my therapist. I have had several starting once I became a teenager, so I will be referring to thoughts and conversations with them from time to time. So yes, I once told my therapist that my parents were neglectful but not intentionally neglectful. He asked me to elaborate on this, and I told him I would have to get back to him. It took me a few days to sit with the statement rolling around in my head and really feel the weight of what I said. So, in the next meeting, we revisited the question\statement, and I had an answer. I took a deep, cleansing breath and started. I told him that my parents did the best with what they had been offered, and that part felt like a copout; however, it was true neither of my parents grew up in a loving, nurturing home. Both of their childhoods were filled with trauma, heartache, and pain.

My grandma Lynn never wanted children, and that showed in how she raised them. And I don't wish to fault Lynn either because her childhood was not all roses and cotton balls. The question for her is, did you not want to end the cycle? Did you not want more for your children once they were here? Did you not love yourself enough in order to love them? My maternal grandmother, Sunny, was part Caucasian, so she had very keen features, big breasts, and a medium tan complexion, which I later learned was a spray tan. She didn't like being too light and had a decent upbringing; however, she got caught up with abusive men and, in turn, left her children with an abusive predator who was three out of her four children's father. So, when I say that my parents did the best that they could with what they had been provided, seen, learned, and experienced, that is true. No, I'm not trying to protect them or give them the benefit of the doubt. I can understand and see their side clearly and understand why things unfolded the way they did. Now, do you remember when I said my childhood wasn't all bad? Amber and Kevin, although not together, held my hands and made me feel secure. I had parents, not Superheroes but parents, adult people who cared for my well-being, my heart, my health, body, and soul. So, when I say unintentional neglect, I mean had it not been for the infection of this drug, my very plain and normal life would not have taken a turn.

Now, once the crack epidemic erupted, we weren't really allowed to play outside, but on the rare occasion, we were allowed to go outside and play. And even though it was in a neighborhood that was riddled with red, black, green, and yellow tops and clear plastic vials that held cracked or broken glass stems, we enjoyed the times we could just go out and be kids. Now the color of the tops represented which crew was selling it, and the crackheads knew by the color of vails if the crack was hitting and giving you the best high. At any time, you could hear corner boys yelling red is out or something like black tops got those black tops. When this epidemic swept through the United States, it swept through like the plague or a hungry wild forest fire, leaving scorched earth behind in its wake. Families would become desolate, destroyed, shattered, and broken. This was a much easier drug to consume and cheaper than heroin. No needles, no tying up your arm or trying to find a worthy vein. For this, all you needed to do was slip some rocks into a small glass pipe, light it on fire, inhale the smoke, and drift off to heaven. The only problem was that the high never lasted long, which led the user to chase that feeling of oblivion. Something that seemed so innocent turned out to be the devil right here on earth. While people tried to keep their composure and to fight from letting the drug take over, they soon found themselves unraveled, turning tricks, robbing, stealing, and lying. Their main focus now was the next fix, the next high, the next elevation to utopia. Crack would be their child, their lover, their friend, their God. Crack is what they cared for, what they nurtured, what they would crave. Now, I can place most of the blame on my Aunt Rose, but the simple fact is that they were all adults and partook in those activities on their own. Crack is the reason why we suffered. This is why we went without. This is why so many families would fray and splinter. Children ripped away from the only homes they ever knew, children born addicted to crack, women self-degrading themselves for the next hit, men selling everything in the household from cable boxes to boxes of cereal, and my mother, father, and James were no different. My parents spun out of control. Their world tilted off its axis as they suffered through their addiction, and their children would suffer silently along with them, our problems never seeming as big or as important as them getting that next hit. So again, intentional but unintentional neglect. How did this unintentional neglect make me feel? Shit small, it made me feel small and insignificant. I would dream of when I once felt secure, and I could barely make myself out in those dreams. Now, what I dreamt of was being forgotten, let down, and abandoned. There was no longer a layer of protection to keep the bad out. The bad was allowed to come straight in, run rampant, and disrupt life anywhere, anytime and anyplace.

When your life is not your own, and you're caught up in the chaos of the adults that are supposed to keep you safe. You learn quickly to fend for yourself and become your own hero. Now, by no means am I saying that my parents completely neglected me, but like I said, neglect is neglect. The funny thing is that my mother, Amber, does not see it like that. She would say, "Stop saying you guys were starving or hungry. You guys ate all the time," and for her, a slice of bread and some black tea or Kool-Aid was eating. Being homeless was never a thing, either. We had a roof over our heads because we never slept on the street. Now, that roof may have been the roof of a car, but she is right. Never did we sleep on the street, so I guess it's all from the perspective of that individual. Now, if you ask Joy and me, we have a completely different take on that, but I guess perception is key, and maybe Amber blocked a lot of the bad things out because she, too, had lived a life of trauma and abuse and never thought that it would trickle down to her children. In some strange way, I think trauma is inherited like it can be passed along the DNA strands. Maybe that is why I tried to break up this trauma when I became a mother. I owed Legend that much for bringing him into a world of hurt, sorrow, and pain. However, I also needed to show him all that the world had to offer: love, laughter, companionship, trust, and loyalty. These are the things my son would be entitled to; this is what I would eventually bring to his table and show him his worth. Because I had to learn that along the way, all on my own. I had no guidance or the quintessential role model. My life was more of a whirlwind of fuck around and find out on your own.

My father, Kevin, could have been one of the many things in my life. He was an exceptional ball player, extremely bright, and had school smarts, street knowledge, and common sense. But his male role models were fucked up. His father died from a heroin overdose, his father's brothers lived down south, his mother's brothers were both spoiled by my great grandma, and they also were addicts. So, Kevin also basically grew up on his own. He never went to school and was constantly getting arrested for graffiti and petty thefts. If only he had someone to pay him just a tiny bit of attention to what he was and wasn't doing, he might have done so much in this life. I love Amber and Kevin with all my heart. They deserved so much more than what they were given by their parents and the people who were supposed to protect them. There is an old saying: once a man, twice a child. I wonder how God will look upon me when he realizes

I have only been a woman and never a child. Sure, I have had brief, fleeting moments of childhood; however, I have had responsibilities because of the condition of my parents. I'm not looking for pity or for you to feel sorry for me. I know I'm not the only person who went through this, but hey, this is my story, and I get to tell you what I want and how it gets told. Now, back to our regularly scheduled discussion of Amber and Kevin. I found it hard being a child not living with both of my parents, having to be absorbed into a family that wasn't mine, and then children being brought forth from different unions. Who did I give my loyalty to? Who did I owe my allegiance to? But none of that matters when both of your parents are addicts. I used to enjoy it when Kevin would pick me up on the weekends. It would make me feel whole like that missing piece could fill my heart for a moment. But as he fell deeper into his addiction and started having other children, the quality time we shared became less, and I became an afterthought. Lost between drugs, new partners, and children, I couldn't compete. I would sometimes sit alone in the window, watching the cars and people go by and pretend that I was with them heading to the zoo or the park. I would replace them with images of my parents.

My only wish was that Amber and Kevin had fought a little harder and stayed together. I can envision that my life would have been remarkably better, and I don't mean material things; I mean unconditional love, care, and nurturing. The bare minimum is all I needed and wanted. Shit, it's still all I want and need from every relationship. However, the cards I had been dealt said that wouldn't be my life and that this would be my testimony. Fate gave me Amber and Kevin. And all the shoulda, woulda, coulda, won't change past events. God gave me this task because he knew I could bear it. He knew that I would succeed. He knew that everything in my life would make me stronger and bring me into the woman I am today. But sometimes just sometimes it's a real struggle to be strong for every one except yourself.

CHAPTER 3: BARELY MAKING IT

Disruption comes at awkward times, and when you least expect it, it is like the devil's hand stirring the pot. A turbulent wind of disruption was approaching, and nearing the midterm of my fourth-grade year, my mother told me we would be moving and that the landlord didn't want us in the building anymore. He had enough of the other tenants complaining about the activities that went on almost every day at all hours of the day. The building was becoming unsafe, and my household was the cause of it. The following day, we packed up what would fit into James' car and stayed at the Marriot across the highway from Morgan Airport. It seems James had got some money. I do not know where he got the money from, and it didn't make a difference to me. It felt like we were on a mini vacation. We didn't have to go to school. We watched cartoons all day and got to eat at McDonald's the whole time we stayed there.

Then, the vacation ended just as abruptly as it had started, and we were living in the station wagon. Do you know how hard it is to live in a car without tinted windows? How degrading it is to have people staring in and pointing at you like you're a zoo exhibit. Or when you need to use the bathroom and must swing the door open, squat down to try and cover up for some form of privacy, and feel the cold breeze hit your backside and send chills up your spine. You start to pray for an ending or a new beginning, and you pray for something better than the current situation. On good nights when my mother and Kevin had extra cash, we would stop at hostels or cheap motels from time to time until my mother got enough courage to ask my grandmother Sunny for aid, and then we made our way to the road and headed toward Chicago. Now, I'm not a stranger to Chicago. I was born there and spent the first two years of my life there, living with my mother and her mother, but I don't remember any of that. Now my maternal grandmother was a wonderful grandma, only because she was a piss-poor mother to her kids, so she made sure to be an excellent grandmother. I guess she was trying to earn brownie points to get into heaven. Maybe she simply saw the wrong she had done to her children and tried to make it better for her grandkids. Who knows? I do hope she made it. I miss her dearly. I digress. We made our way to Wakefield, Chicago, where my grandmother had a store called the "Waab." We would frequent that store almost daily. Now Sunny had a church friend who lived in Deer Park and had a furnished basement apartment for rent.

In this basement, we were supposed to be renting once my mother obtained a job, so the church sister, Ms. Parker, was simply giving us a pass on the strength of my grandmother, Sunny, from whom I got my first name. Her middle name is my first. Now Sunny assured Ms. Parker that her daughter and family were God-loving, God-fearing, obedient, quiet, and good people and that she would not even know we were present. I have to laugh at this because, Lord, we lasted about two months before good old church-going sister Parker lost her religion and cursed James and my mother out and not so sisterly put us out for all the late-night traffic. Now Deer Park crackheads are a little different than New Brunswick crackheads. They are almost country, in the sense that you would think we were in a backwater town in Georgia and not in a state under New Brunswick that had missing teeth, was extra rowdy, and just countrified as all outdoors. Well, with the ruckus, racket, and unwanted negative attention, we brought to that poor lady's door. So, my mother called my grandma Sunny to bail us out. Sunny came to our rescue, mad and fuming, but Sunny paid for us to be in a motel called the Sea Breeze Motel, found on the Blue Bird Turnpike between Deer Park and Wakefield, right at the borderline. This little strip is where you came when you wanted the excitement of Deer Park; however, you couldn't afford the boardwalk prices. It has a little inlet with a small beach, a Hess gas station that doubled as a bodega, and two holes-in-the-wall restaurants whose names I cannot remember for the life of me. Maybe because we never went into them.

Now Sunny paid for us to stay at the Sea Breeze for roughly a month, and then we would have to make our own way. This led to James breaking down and calling his father Mr. Big. He served in WWII and, after the war, moved up to New Brunswick from Alabama. He had gotten in good with some Italians and opened a number spot in the back of his diner on 123rd and 8th Avenue. Mr. Big would now take on the responsibility of paying for the Sea Breeze for the entire length of time we stayed there and about four times a year take us clothes and food shopping. Now, my mother, Amber, secured a job at the Sea Breeze as a house cleaner. It is easy to work, and it helped keep their addiction afloat.

Sometimes, the owners, Mr. Seth and his wife, would give me my own assignment and let me clean rooms. This would actually come in handy since there were times when my mother and James had no money, and we had no food. I had asked Mr. Seth to hold all my earnings in case of emergency. They were a lovely family, so he did so with no problem. I honestly think he used to add money to my little pot because he knew the situation we had been in. We would use my earnings to get food from time to time. Now, the supermarket was in Watersplace, about a mile and a half from the Sea Breeze, and we would walk there and back because James was too busy to drive us. Busy doing what I don't know, only God knows, we did this carrying multiple bags of groceries through all types of weather. These walks are why I love walking now. At the time, I had no other choice but to walk. And now I walk almost everywhere.

Now, the Sea Breeze motel was composed of two sides: its main side, which ran all year long, and the summer side with a pool, which only opened in the summer. Of course, we lived on the side that ran all year long on the second floor in one of the three kitchenette rooms they had. It was like a small one-bedroom apartment. Joy and I had the bedroom, and James and my mother had the living room.

Now, changing from the inner city broad of education in New Brunswick to the kind of suburban, mainly white schools of Bell Harbor Township was strange, to say the least, and having to explain to my teachers and classmates that I lived in a motel with my mom, stepdad, and siblings was terrifying, so I embellished the truth and told everyone that we were having work done on our house. It was safer for us to stay there. This harmless lie worked for about half the fifth-grade school year, and then people just stopped asking me. I guess they figured I was embarrassed and let it drop. They had more important things to worry about other than why I lived in a motel on the strip. What I will say about the school system there is that, at the time, it was excellent. By the time I returned to the eighth grade in New Brunswick, I was on a tenth-grade level and would have become the valedictorian, but I had not been in the school for the entire junior high school experience.

For the most part, Joy and I were stuck in this kitchenette and barely went outside, so we would manufacture games that we could play inside or think extremely out of the box. We would pretend we were world-class tango dancers or door-to-door sales ladies. One day, in particular, Joy wanted to swing. We didn't live near a park, and there were no activities for children on the motel property, so I tied one end of a rope around Joy and the other to the radiator, lowered her out the window, and let her swing outside of the window. I spun her around a few times and told her I'd be right back in a minute. I needed to use the bathroom. Upon leaving the bathroom, I walked into the kitchen for some water and then sat in the front with my mother, totally forgetting about Joy. I had been sitting with my mother for what seemed like ten minutes when she asked me where Joy was. When it dawned on me that I had left her dangling outside of the window, I jumped up and ran into the back to pull her back inside. I didn't know that my mother was on my heels and had followed me into the back. She had quietly and patiently waited for me to finish pulling Joy in, who was upset that I was pulling her in, yelling if I could leave her out for a little longer. God only knows what she was doing hanging on the side of the motel. Once Joy's feet hit the floor, I hit the floor with her. Amber knocked me out. I don't know if she said anything or kept hitting me. What I do know is that my head hurt for a whole week after this incident, and you can trust and believe I never hung her, or anyone for that matter, out of a window again. After this incident, I would torment Joy.

I did mean and hateful things to her, so maybe that's why I spoil her now. I would make her eat food from off the floor with bugs on it. I would lock her in a closet, knowing she feared the dark. I gave her toilet water to drink, telling her it was from the tap. I would just pick on her until she got fed up with me and eventually ended up stabbing me with a pencil in my right middle finger. When I think back to that day, I had just gotten her (Joy) in trouble for kicking the glass out of the door, and Amber gave her a beating. Joy was so mad she grabbed that damn He-Man pencil and stabbed me right in my hand when I yelped; I was actually in shock that Joy fought back. Amber came out, and Joy immediately said I tripped and fell, which was totally possible since I'm a klutz. My mother pulled the pencil out of my finger, slapped me, and told us to go sit the hell down. I sit back and laugh at days like this. Even in my protective state of being a surrogate parent, I still tried to have some sort of childhood with my sister. Nowadays, Joy is my annoying best friend, and ain't nobody allowed to fuck with her or hurt her feelings. Because she is dramatic, erratic, and loud, she calls me with all her problems, and I don't have the time for it. Like I've told you, I have six biological siblings. However, the relationship between Joy and I is something worthy of a book of its own. My little big sister, when she became a mother and beat me to it, sure she stumbled and fumbled along the way; however, she rebounded, and I'm in awe of her and all she has accomplished.

Joy stands on business and is always ten toes down. She had amazing people to look up to on her father's side of the family, and surprisingly, she credits me as one of her role models, so I must have done something right. Joy is not my favorite sibling, as many believe, because she truly irks my nerves. In fact, all of them get on my nerves, and maybe that's just a little sibling thing where they are supposed to irk your nerves and drive you to the brink of sanity; however, those are my babies, and I will go to war for each one of them. They are me, and I'm them, and that will always be an unbreakable bond. Joy and I have the absolute best big-sister-little sister relationship. She gets on my nerves religiously; everything is code red, level ten chaos in her world, and everything needs solving right there on the spot. And, of course, I'm always there to make sure we have a solution to her latest issue. Putting out her fires has become a favorite pastime of mine. I wouldn't have it any other way, except when she is being completely unreasonable and ignoring my feelings like I'm a robot and made of computer chips.

Joy is spoiled, and it's not that I haven't contributed to that. My sisters and brothers were my children and, to some extent, still are. Normally, when they call, I come running. Now, for Joy, every birthday since I've had a real paying job, I make sure it's special. I don't do that for my other siblings; however, I just make sure they are reasonably healthy and taken care of. Joy is special. Maybe it's because she is my first sibling\child or because she's the closest one of my siblings to me. I truly love them all equally. However, Joy holds a special spot and always will. As children, as I mentioned before, I would torture her because I was upset that she had become my responsibility when I had no clue about how to handle someone at such a young age. It truly wasn't her fault. It was the environment we were given and had to endure. As our parents slowly and then rapidly spiraled out of control, I became the head of household, the unwilling head of household. What a shame and what a burden that had been placed on my shoulders, and even though I didn't like Joy at that point, I did it with a smile. What else could I do? I had to hold us together; I didn't want BCW to come in and rip us apart. Who knows where and what we would end up with? I figured living with our parents would be the best possible option for us, and I have to say I was right because six out of my six siblings are doing just fine.

Chapter 4: Fire

Now, in the time that we lived at the Sea Breeze, my mother would go on to have two sons, Jet and Jim. They are 13 months apart, and that's called being Irish Twins, or so I believe. By the time Jet had turned on the side of the Sea Breeze, we had been living in a place caught on fire one late at night. Now, you may think I'm crazy about this next part; however, I swear an ancestor saved my family and me that night. We watched Nightmare on Elm Street, and once the movie was done, Joy and I went to sleep in the bedroom. I had such a vivid dream that night that even to this day, it is clear and easy to recall. In this dream, an Indian Chief floating in the air was telling me no, urging me to get up, and yelling at me to save them. I could not for the life of me figure out who they were, so I continued to argue with the chief when he landed in front of me, took me by the shoulders, and shook me so hard that I woke up and in a sleepy haze I stared at the floor and started to swirl my hand through the thick black smoke that was about ankle high for about a minute I got up went to the bathroom and got back in the bed before I realized what was happening.

Oh my God, there was a fire somewhere in the motel. I jumped up and ran into the living room, where my mother, James, and my younger brothers slept. I tried to wake my mother up by calling her name, screaming mommy, and shaking her, but she didn't budge, so I bit her. She reacted to that by slapping the shit outta me, and I screamed FIRE! While holding my face, she jumped up and ran into the kitchen to check the stove, but there was nothing. She yelled for James to grab the boys. She ran into the back and grabbed Joy. As we exited the room, I ran through the whole motel, knocking and banging on doors and screaming, "Fire, fire," when we reached the lower level, I ran to the owners' room and woke them up. They called 911. In the early morning of March 25th, 1991, the motel was engulfed in bright red and orange flames. It was beautiful to watch as the flames seemed to dance and talk to each other to see whose flame could go the highest. No, I'm not a fire starter or a pyromaniac. I see the beauty in all things. It's strange to see something in its raw and natural form. By the time the fire department arrived, much of the motel was already in a blaze. Once the fire was extinguished, the sun was up, and all the occupants of the Sea Breeze Motel were huddled together in the wintry morning, looking lost to the world. Fortunately, the Seths opened the summer side of the motel and allowed us to stay there. As we started heading to the other side, news reporters stopped us and interviewed James and me. It was the first time I was ever on television or interviewed; this was the first time I felt special and noticed.

I returned to school about a week after the fire. My school was predominantly white in Bell Harbor Township, called PS 58. There were bundles of clothes and boxes of food that the community had collected on behalf of the families affected by the fire. We didn't stay at the Sea Breeze much longer. I finished out the seventh grade, and we moved back to New Brunswick. Mr. Big got us an apartment on 123rd Street and Eighth Ave. He paid the rent for us. My mother got food stamps, and my father, from time to time, would give her money for me, so that's how we survived for the time being.

That summer, my mother enrolled Joy and me in the Police Athletic League, which at the time was right across the street from where we lived. That summer, I won MS. PAL for my essay on why I enjoyed PAL. I spoke from the heart. It's funny that I have never had a problem putting my thoughts and feelings to paper. Yet, speaking in public, I would sometimes get tongue-tied. I spoke about being free from drama and not having to worry about meals, hearing my mother and James fight and argue, having strangers coming in and out of the house praying they would leave without causing an uproar, and being around peers who could relate to me and could provide a listening ear. And having anywhere besides home that felt like home.

That summer, I reconnected with my father and his side of the family. It had been almost three years since I last saw my father and that side of my family. Reconnecting with them filled a small void that I didn't know I had been missing. You know that saying Daddy's little girl never really applied to his relationship with me. I was just happy to be around my family. And if he stayed around, I was happy for him to be there, too. Had my father not been an addict in one form or another throughout my life, he would have been an excellent father despite his lack of guidance and love that he never received. He has always tried to give more than he received. However, his habits kept him from reaching his full potential for himself and his children. My father now has two other children, Kevin Jr and Gabby. They share the same mother, Nicole. Nicole was an addict as well. I mean, man, I cannot get a break like all my parental figures have fallen prey to this scourge called Crack. And because of their drug use, they would eventually end up losing custody of Kevin Jr. and Gabby. The good thing is they ended up with Nicole's mother, Mrs. Bell, so they remained close in the family. Our father would pick them up and bring them over to Lynn or my aunt Janet's house for the day or weekend, and sometimes he would scoop me up with them. He would drop us off and, most of the time, be gone until it was time to take us home.

Staying with my younger siblings at Lynn's house was horrible. My grandmother's house was roach-infested and void of love. The only good thing was that the girls lived there, but the apartment was not a home. It was cold and rigid. My grandmother is likened to a dictator. One would only be useful if they could provide her with what she needed at that time. The bright side of things was the bond I was developing with my siblings and cousins, or when my father would stay around long enough so we could go outside to the park and get away from the roaches and the evil that is Lynn. This was the norm until Kevin went to jail, and Mrs. Bell started to keep them from us. She didn't want them to know our father had gone to prison, and as an adult, I can now understand that. As a child, I was pissed cause all I knew was that my brother and sister were being kept away from me. And, of course, as I was with my mother's children, I was the same way with my father's children: mother hen to the rescue, and I tried to keep in touch with them. I even scaled the wall to where their grandmother lived to try and see them, but she called security on me and had me removed from the property. Then I started calling and leaving nasty messages until I eventually stopped and prayed that they would find me when they were older.

At the summer's end, my mother enrolled me in Phillip Green Middle School. So that I could complete my eighth-grade year. Being back in New Brunswick was a culture shock. I had not been in a predominantly African American school since the fourth grade. These kids, my peers, were in no way blind to my situation; however, there was no need to speak about it because the majority of us were in the same situation, and it was a shared unspoken truth among us. A common thread between us linked us, so there was no one better than the next, and we were equals. It felt good to be around people who knew your story and wouldn't judge you. I fit in, I fit in, and there were no explanations needed, no showboating, no masks or facades. I could we could all be ourselves. As I went along in eighth grade, we started a little hustle where we would get candy and sell it to people in school on the trains, parks, and buses anywhere and wherever. Someone was always willing to buy those candy bars. Yes, we did this in the 90s, well before "It's Showtime" on the trains became a popular thing. Or when the school gave us those damn boxes of chocolates to sell, we either kept the chocolate or we sold them and kept the money. Of course, you couldn't sell it in the area where you lived, so we would walk to 86th Street and peddle our chocolate there. My group\gang of candy thieves was the

Phillip Green chess club, the same group of kids that stayed after school to learn how to play chess. Yeah, I guess I was a bit of a nerd. Selling the candies allotted me some money in my pockets that my mother and James didn't know about so I could get Joy Jet and Jim snacks and sandwiches to hold us over during the night. If you asked my brothers, they didn't know we were poor and mainly living off the virtuousness of their grandparents, James, mother Anne, and we already know his father, Mr. Big. They paid the rent in the apartment we lived in, and my mother got welfare, but James's addiction had really become out of control. So, his parents financially kept us together. Thank goodness for his parents PAL and school, or we would have been in a world of trouble. James would sell almost anything in that house that wasn't nailed down to feed his addiction. The one thing I'm grateful for is that Jet and Jim don't really recall all the hardships until their father, James, got sick from cancer and died. Would you believe he was walking around with an oxygen tank still coping crack? Yes, it was that bad. I guess at that point, he had figured if I'm going to die, I might as well be high. By this time, my mother started weaning herself off of the drug and was getting her footing back. Years of drug use had stolen her shape and fucked up her face by picking her skin, but when I look at her, I always see the shapely beautiful Amber she was before drugs came to be a part of her life.

When I was graduating from junior high school, Kevin, my father, who, despite his addictions, always kept a job, took me shopping for my dress and shoes. My mother hot combed my hair with this torture device that looked like a comb, but it sat on the stove until the arms on it turned from black to fire engine red. That's when you knew it was hot enough to pass through your hair. I know a lot of young black girls can relate to this. The smell of grease and burnt hair filled the apartment on 8th Ave, but my hair was soft, thick, and long. I had never seen it like that. It flowed down my back like an onyx waterfall. Man, a few scabs behind my ear didn't matter because the hot comb was touching my skin. I was fixing to fly for the first time ever. I received so many awards that year, and it gave me an ego boost that I desperately needed. The nice pressout didn't last but three days, and the June heat and my sweat had me running around looking like Don King, so my mother, who cannot do hair to save her life, put my hair in dodo plats, you know three huge braids with uneven parts. Mind you, I'm soon to go to ninth-grade high school, still running around like Ms. Celia from The Color Purple. No big deal. I'm a kid enjoying my summer before having to be a high school student.

CHAPTER 5: HIGH SCHOOL

On the first day of the school year, as a high school student, I was nervous, but I looked decent. I had on some brown stirrup leggings, a black, white, and brown button-down shirt, and some black Nike sneakers. All thanks to Kevin. Oh, and my hair. The downstairs neighbor put it in two tight, neat French braids for my mother because Amber somehow hurt her wrist. Anyway, I arrived at Health Professions and Human Services. Found the old beauty school on 15th and 1st Ave extra early. The doors hadn't even opened yet. Amber wanted to make sure I got to school on time, and since it was downtown, she made me leave early, saying something about travel time and rush-hour traffic. Now, this school was for all the smart kids who didn't make it into one of those specialized high schools where you have to take a test to get in, so we were smart, just not that smart. Now, around 7:15, teachers started to arrive and felt bad for me, so they let me wait inside. Around 8 am, students started to arrive, and it was one of the most beautiful things I had ever seen. The sea of colors, shapes, and sizes was startling. I had never seen so many different people coming together in one place. This school was nothing like the other schools I had attended. The schools in Chicago serviced a large population of whites, and the schools in New Brunswick serviced mainly people of color. Not HPHS, Asian, White, Black Spanish, Indian, you name it, they were present, and I knew for sure I would fit in, which I did with a group of kids that weren't cool but cool, not nerds but nerds, we were kind of outsiders that were included with the cool kids. Quick sidebar we were the first entering class and graduating class of HPHS, so the school started with only ninth graders, so we all pretty much knew everyone from the jocks to the emo kids to the yearbook club. The school was easy enough for me to navigate all my classes except gym. I don't have a physical bone in my body except for volleyball.

I failed gym every semester and every year while in high school, and to make it up, I always took a science class because I love science well until the last semester of senior year when I failed math because I had started to cut class and hang out with an older boy that would get me pregnant I'd keep it to myself not even telling him and taking care of it myself all by myself to have a two-day abortion because I was almost 4 months, back to the time frame of ninth grade. I had a few friends from Phillip Green who attended HPHS with me, so there was a feeling of familiarity present; however, that didn't last too long. They would branch off and join their own clicks except for one Luz, fair complexion, 5'6 long, stringy black hair a little on the chubby side. She lived on 145th and Broadway. Her family is originally from Singapore. Luz also had a friend from her block who attended HPHS with us. So, she would become my friend too. Actually, she would become my best friend in HPHS, which sucks because we aren't close at all now, but people grow up and grow apart, and not everyone is supposed to remain in your circle. Now Luz, myself, and Gina, who had shoulder-length blondish color hair, large front teeth, no shape, and a wide ass. The three of us hung out the most. Outta the little click we had and to spend more time together, we would walk from 1st Ave to 7th Ave to catch the 1 or 9 trains. I got off on 103rd, and they both got off on 145th. Luz and Gina both made me feel like I had real friends. I never divulged my deepest, darkest secrets to them, but I felt comfortable enough to speak about my day-to-day chaos, which was always good for a good laugh. Always talking about the nonsense Lynn did or the shenanigans that went on in my family. Funny thing, they never really told me about their lives. Sure, Gina told us she lived with her brother and his wife because her parents had died tragically, but besides that, nothing, and Luz, which I knew even longer, I knew even less.

Now, do you folks remember me saying my father's family plays a huge role in my life? Well, there is a turn of events coming up that explains why I say this. My father would normally call and say he was stopping by or that he wanted me for the weekend, but I guess he felt he didn't need to call on this day, and he rang the bell and wanted me to come downstairs. Now, normally, James never had a problem with my father, but I guess something was in the air because James came down like a bull and tackled my father. They wrestled a little bit, and someone called the cops. They both went to jail and were released shortly after that. Now, these are guys who have gotten high together, laughed and joked around together, and shared meals, but for whatever reason, that hot day in the spring, temperatures were hot. And so were they. Now, shortly after this incident, during spring break of my ninth-grade school year, my father's sister Janet, the one whose middle name is my middle name, a tall, dark-skinned, beautiful, and an unstoppable force once she set her mind to something that was it, and her husband, Ralph. The humblest man I have ever met. He and his family all have these trademark slanted eyes that make you think they have more than just Native American in them. Well, they stopped by my apartment on 123rd and summoned me to come downstairs. Now, this was strange because she literally lived five blocks and two avenues away from me, and this was the first time I could recall her coming over without being called over. Little secret: I was scared of my aunt. She was very tough and would fight at the drop of a dime, but she was funny and loving and didn't play about her family, so when I saw her downstairs, I was excited. James came downstairs, and Janet Ralph and James talked for a few minutes. I really wasn't paying their conversation any attention; I was sitting on the stoop steps in my own thoughts when I heard Janet say, "nigga, that's my mother fucking niece, and if I wanna take her, ain't shit, you gonna do or say to me." My head spun around so fast I think I got whiplash. I wanted to see this fight. I just knew Janet was going to kick James's ass. I was secretly praying she would kick his ass for all the times he made Amber cry. James looked like he was getting into a stance, and Janet flared her nostrils and said, "Go ahead, nigga, and I will be the last thing you ever see." I don't know if she was serious, but James backed down. She then turned to Ralph and told him to get a cab. She looked at me and said, "Monique, get up. We are leaving." James said, "No, she isn't," and reached out to grab me; however, Janet was fast and grabbed me and pulled me to the curb, so when the cab pulled up, she literally threw me in and the cab and took me to Lynn's house. So, I essentially had been kidnapped by my aunt and taken away from my mother and siblings. Who would protect them if I weren't there? Who would make sure they had everything they needed to survive? This event would become a great source of anxiety and fear for me.

Janet said, "Look, you ain't going back there. You are staying with grandma and the girls now." The girls are two of her four daughters, Ellie and Michi. Janet had six kids, and she was busy. The four girls, Ellie, Michi, Kim, and Alaya, and two boys, Mase and Jov. The girls literally taught me how to dress and gave me a swagger. They have always been cool, beautiful, and effortlessly DOPE. How couldn't I model myself and my sense of style after them? My cousins kinda molded me into a hip nerd, and I would suck up as much as I could from them, and once I perfected it, I added my own little flare to it and made it my own. So, we've already met Michi in this story. Now Ellie is my big cousin, but if you ask her, we are the same age because we both were born in 79, but her birthday is June, and mine is October and last I checked, June comes before October, so big cousin Ellie it is. Ellie, also a beautiful dark-skinned girl with flawless skin approximately my height or maybe just a few inches shorter than me, either rocked a fly short haircut or box braids. Moving in with the girls, my aunt Shonda, and her son Dash was a tight fit in Lynns' three-bedroom apartment, but it felt good to be around my father's family now from the age of fourteen till about nineteen I lived here no more visiting I was an official resident of Eagle Edge projects. Shonda, when I was younger, was dope. She had a fly shape and kept her hair and nails on point. She was the color of smooth, warm caramel with a gap in her teeth that actually heightened her look. It gave her a little of an edgy look when paired with red lipstick, but now she's washed up and washed out. Dash, my younger bratty cousin the color of a toffee candy with a big egg-shaped head, was spoiled beyond belief, and that would trickle into his adult life, but hey, this book ain't about him.

In Eagle Edge, I would become an alcoholic, get pregnant a few times, and look for love in all the wrong places because love wasn't given at home, more like the shock incarceration I resided in. My cousins and I would run away from home and join a gang called the Claw, and with this incurable bad behavior, I almost didn't make it out of high school. A bright spot is that I would get my first real job with the then Bold program now known as Lefrak Children's Zone. Living in Eagle Edge wasn't all bad. I learned how to cook and made some great friends that I still hang out with from time to time. I had a sense of freedom that I never had with my mother. I was able to go out more often and travel around as long as I was back by curfew.

Sometimes, Lynn would tell the girls and me to come to check in at seven, and we would. Then she would tell us to rest our nerves, and I never understood what that meant, but I gather it was her adult way of saying y'all keep your asses in this house and stop with all the back and forth. But for three young teenage girls coming up in the 90s, this was heartbreaking. Our friends would still be outside having fun, but on slow days, they would come to sit in the hallway with us to keep us company. They would end up doing this a lot because we were almost always on punishment. Now that I lived with my father's family, I tried to balance seeing my mother, siblings, and school. But it soon became very hard, so for birthdays and holidays, I would be present. Around this time, I actually started to build up some resentment for my aunt Janet, not because she kidnapped me but because she took me from my siblings. Which made it harder for me to keep my eyes on them and make sure they were safe; however, you know the world is always turning, so a new event was bubbling up on the horizon. Lynn would punish and beat me for coming in late because I would consistently come in late from checking in on my mother and siblings. The beatings and the punishments didn't detour me from the mission I put myself on, for I had made this promise, this oath to keep them safe and protected, and I did this to the very best of my ability. Unfortunately, this oath and this promise would eventually burn me out and make me a little bitter; however, I'd make this decision repeatedly if I ever had to.

CHAPTER 6: THE ACCIDENT

In the summer of June 1995, I was actually pretty sharp. My father took me to shop for clothes and got my hair permed (worst thing ever) So I'd be ready for the upcoming start of 11th grade. A new hairstyle and fresh gear gave me the confidence I had been lacking. Now, on my cousin Ellie's sixteenth birthday, June 21st, which means I was still fifteen, my father and I were at his best friend's house. It was a beautiful, warm June night. He and Bobby Black had been drinking and smoking weed from early afternoon well into the night, and when my father was ready, he called for me to come downstairs.

I had been upstairs with Bobby's family. I came downstairs and got into his car. He turned to me and said, "Put your seatbelt on," then waited for me to do so before he pulled off, and what seemed like a few seconds after that, we would get into a car accident. Two correction officers crashed into the right passenger side of the car. They hit us with so much force that they propelled the motorcycle they were on over the car and approximately 150 feet from the car. My father turned toward me and asked if I was good. I shook my head, and he took off. He said he was heading to the police station. I'd like to believe that's where he was heading, but I really don't know what was actually going on in his head. Remember, he had been drinking and getting high for the better part of the afternoon. Unbeknownst to us, a car followed us and called the police, which then turned into a police chase.

When my father finally pulled over, he handed me the bag of weed he had and said to hide it. I put in my bra. I wasn't thinking about them searching me or that I could get into trouble. I just didn't want my father to be in any more trouble than he was already. Back at the scene, we ended up leaving one person dead and the other badly injured, becoming a paraplegic. He would later die from his drug addiction. Sidebar: both the corrections officers had cocaine in their systems. So, this wasn't just my father's fault. It was all that was involved while driving under the influence. However, my father would end up going to prison, not jail, and being sentenced to two consecutive sentences of 4-8 years.

With my father gone, the buffer in my grandmother's house was gone. He was the only person who stood between me and Lynn. He was my protection in that apartment, and he was not in prison, and no one paid attention to the orphan of the house unless they needed something from me. My grandmother Lynn would basically turn Ellie, Michi, and myself into her personal servants, one cleaning the bathroom, one in the living room, and the other in the kitchen. If you had the kitchen, you had to cook. For her own personal needs, one had to clip her toenails and massage her feet, the other had to scratch her scalp and grease it, and the other had to rub and massage her legs. This was her everyday routine when she came home from work, and if you were on punishment, then you did all her personal care by yourself. She never lifted a finger in that apartment. Why would she when she had servants? And I know y'all like, what's the problem? She gave y'all chores, but if the chores weren't done to her satisfaction, she'd beat us or punish us. Lynn was just miserable and wanted everyone around her to be miserable as well. Anyway, I think I said this already, but I was the best cook out of the three, so I stayed in the kitchen. I didn't mind cooking. It was relaxing at the time, but now I hate cooking.

With Kevin being sent to prison, I'd soon to spiral into my own tailspin, but I'd eventually pull out of it and land on my feet. You know that strong black, hyper-independent woman is just around the corner. I can't become my parents. Shit, that was and is my worst fear!

Entering HPHS, I knew all the eleventh graders and got to know some of the new ninth graders; however, I remained with my crew, the cool but not-so-cool kids, and that was ok because I felt comfortable around them, not enough to tell them my life story but enough to laugh and joke with. I never attended school events because, one, I didn't have money, and two, no one ever asked me to go to prom, no school dances, no field trips, no extracurricular activities, nothing. Part of the tailspin and a large contributing factor to my tailspin was the boys.

Chapter 7: Boys

Then came the Boys. Fifteen and sixteen is the time boys and men started to notice me without needing a hookup. I know I said I was cute, and you couldn't tell me anything, but I never looked at myself as beautiful or attractive. I always felt like guys liked me because I was a black girl with real hair or because my cousins were the cool ones, so they didn't want to leave me out. So, when men and boys would approach me, this was something new and exciting. A boost to my low self-esteem. At one point, I had a sex book with the names and ages of everyone I slept with or had some kind of sexual encounter with. Y'all wanna know, don't you? Well, it was more than eight and less than twenty now. The thing about me is momma told me don't shit where you eat, so the majority of my sexcapades weren't in Eagle Edge. Sure, I spoke with and dated people from Eagle Edge, but they weren't giving me a chance to take part in sexual activities with my shit. I do have some kind of morals.

(Sidebar: my top five complete sexual encounters are Sam, Raymond, Noah, Mel, and Ben, in no particular order) Now, I'm not saying that I was a hoe, but I was a hoe and I'm admitting it. I liked the attention that came from it. The sad thing about that is I didn't have the guidance to tell me love was not between my legs or in bullshit pickup lines from guys that wanted to put notches on their belts, but if they paid attention to what was in my head or tried to elevate me mentally emotionally and spiritually that was love and the attention that I needed. However, I would have to learn the hard way. Ok, I'll let you know how many guys from Eagle Edge or the surrounding ten blocks and three avenues over in either direction. As a teenager, I slept with four, not including Sam. His family is from Eagle Edge. However, he was born in Rockland County. And as an adult, three. Now, don't ask about my overall number because that isn't any of your business nosy.

In tenth grade, I started to cut class and hang out with these men and boys, allowing them to use my body because I thought they liked me or loved me. Remember, I was told this is how a man shows a woman he loves her at eight, and no, it wasn't like I was fucking ten random dudes a day; however, if we were, and I use this term lightly, dating more than likely, you was getting this good Honeepot. Yes, I know I spelled Honeepot wrong, but that's my name for my good "good." mind your business. I'm joking. Continue reading. Men used sex just for notches in their belts. I used it to feel loved and connected. I needed to feel like I was chosen, seen, and wanted. Again, looking for love in all the wrong places.

My parents were absentee parents. My grandmother didn't care about me unless someone was giving her money so I could live with her. My aunt Shonda was busy with her son Dash and the many men she entertained. Now Shonda is a whore. There is a difference in the hood between a whore and a hoe, and she learned how to be a whore from my grandmother. A hoe was just having sex to have sex, but a whore was getting paid for her goods. Shit, it is the oldest profession in the world, so why the hell not. Don't get me wrong, they both had jobs and worked, but they also had Wild African Americans tricking on them. They used what they had to get whatever they wanted. Great role models, right? Maybe I should have been a whore instead. I tell you, baby, I really had to save myself. Now, my favorite aunt on my father's side, Janet, even though I was scared of her, was busy trying to get her life back on track for herself and her kids. I was extremely proud of her for making strides to be better. It's an accomplishment coming from the house she grew up in. I think that's why I would give my father and them so much grace. They lived with a monster, and now, I live with her. Living in Lynn's house wasn't much better than staying in a shelter. I might have fared better off staying with my mother and siblings, but I thought I was choosing up. Yes, I lived with my cousins. However, I was the odd one out because they're sisters, so they have a sisterly bond.

Now get this straight: my cousins love me and would rock out for me if needed, but they had their own traumas that they were dealing with. You may ask, what about my siblings? Yes, my mother's children were there, but they couldn't give me the love that I desperately sought from my own parents. They were children themselves. Dealing with the crappy life they were born into as well. So, I sought out love in all the wrong places and from all the wrong people. Remember, I had been violated at a tender and impressionable age and never had someone to tell me that those actions and words that had been imprinted into my heart, soul, and mind weren't true. They were nothing more than ugly actions that would keep me shackled and trapped in my own feelings, allowing things that no self-respected girl lady or woman would allow.

In the spring of 1995, just before Kevin went to prison, my cousin Ellie set me up with a wild African American named Amare. So, they never got a chance to meet. But honestly, when we were 15, who would think years later we'd link back up and become an item? Anyway, Ellie was dating Amare's best friend at the time, Sabastian. Amare was handsome in a very boyish kind of way; he had dark brown eyes, an athletic build but on the slimmer side, big, soft, plush lips, and a big camel nose. We surely didn't hit it off well on my part at first. He seemed a little too into me, and for my life, I couldn't understand why. Well, Amare and Sabastian would come down to our grandmothers' house to either sit in the park with us or sit in the damn hallway because Lynn was not letting them in the house shit. She barely wanted us there. Anyway, I was usually very mean and snotty to Amare. I wasn't really giving him any play, and he tried his hardest every single time he came over. And I would constantly reject him, his gifts, his hugs, his attempts to kiss me. Everything he did was completely wrong. I was so mean to Amare. I have no idea why he stuck around. Maybe it was because I rejected him, so he felt the need to take me down. Lord knows I would have said kick rocks, you stuck-up bitch. However, he persisted and eventually

51

showed up at my grandmother's by himself. He had sunflowers and a big ass teddy bear, and of course, I was treating him like shit, and I guess he was fed up. Amare said fuck you, I'm outta here and started to walk toward the elevator. I couldn't believe he was leaving me. I called out to him. Tears suddenly welled up in my eyes, and I took off after him, grabbed him, and kissed him with my entire soul. And for the first time, I looked at him, and something changed inside of me. The tears I had been holding back fell, and I opened up to him. I cried on his shoulder and told him about all my troubles, wants, needs, and disappointments. He held my face and kissed my tear-stained face, told me I was the most beautiful girl in the world and that I was gonna be his wife. The funny thing is I believed him.

Amare was a street dude, so trying to stay in contact was damn near impossible. It was always by happenstance that I'd call his place, and his dad would tell me to hold on and call him on the phone. and I would call almost three times every single day. But when he was there, we would stay on the phone for hours; shoot, he would even listen to me sleep. We stayed on the phone for so long that my grandmother and his father told us to use the pay phone. God, that made trying to stay in touch with each other even harder. Amare has a cousin who's older and has his own place. Let's call him Moe. Well, Amare gave me Moe's number and said to start calling him there every Tuesday around 5, and like the lovesick teen I was, I did as told, and we would just talk until my quarters ran out and plan the next time we'd see each other. And the warmth I felt as soon as he was in my eyesight was unexplainable. It's almost like I was radiating heat the closer he got to me. This is some crazy chemistry. And once finally in his arms, I'd melt. He once said my face lit up like a kid on Christmas morning, and that was one of the things he liked most about me, you know, after I stopped being a bitch to him. Amare's visits started to become very infrequent, and the calls would become sporadic.

I hadn't heard from or seen him in months, but one day, he called and told me to come over to his cousin Moe's house, and of course, I did. I was super excited to see him. I told my cousin to go with me because I didn't want to go by myself. She and Sabastian weren't really fucking with each other either, but she knew how desperate I was to see Amare, so she humored me and tagged along. Amare was standing in front of Moe's building, waiting for us. I ran up to him and kissed him fully on his lips. I had really missed him. I hadn't realized how much he meant to me. Was I falling in love with him? Possibly, however, I'd deal with that emotion later right now in the present tense. I'm with him, and that's all that matters. Ellie asked if Sabastian was upstairs, and Amare said yea, so we followed him into the building and up the steps. Inside Moe's crib was a typical bachelor pad junky but not messy random dudes smoking weed, drinking, and chopping it up. Amare took my hand and led me into one of the rooms. We sat on the bed and talked, no touching, no kissing, nothing but catching up when he touched my face and said Monique, I love you, and for the first time, I said it back to him. We had been dating for about a year, and he faithfully told me he loved me, but this night, I said it back, and we started kissing and heavy petting, and the next thing I knew, we were connected as one making a baby. Amare was very long and girthy. So, when he entered me, I let out a little yell. He kissed me and said baby, keep it down. They'll hear us. I had forgotten that there were people in the house, and honestly, I didn't care. I was consumed by the heat I felt in my stomach and the racing of my heart. I was young and felt like I was in love, feeling all kinds of emotions and sparks of energy coursing through my body. I gave in to this pleasure and built-up pressure, and my damn burst, and I flooded the bed. It was magically we came at the same time as he lay on top of me, both breathing heavily like we had just run a marathon. Amare started kissing my face and telling me I was his forever, and I felt that deep in my soul. No, I never rated Amare because Amare wasn't just sex. We made love every single time, no quickies, no fucking, always gentle and passionate, and no one, and I mean no one, can compare to what Amare does to me.

Amare and Sabastian walked Ellie and me to the bus, waited for us to board, and then went back to Moe's. Well, at least that's what they said. While riding the bus, I told Ellie I slept with Amare, and she said yea bitch, the whole house knows y'all was fucking. I felt a little embarrassed, but oh well, that's my man, and I love my man. I know I know I love everyone, but Amare was and is completely different from everyone including Sam. The following weekend, Amare and Sabastian came to pick Ellie and me up and take us to the movies. You know, I was excited, and Ellie was too. She and Sabastian were back on good terms. Unfortunately, an unfortunate turn of events would occur and fracture my relationship with Amare. Sabastian had been dating Amare's cousin, and she and her friends happened to get on the same train as the four of us, so he came up with the bright idea to act like he and Amare were playing fighting, and when the train doors were about to close, they fell out of the train. So unbeknownst to Ellie and I got off at the next stop and waited like assholes for them to come. We let two trains go by, thinking that they would be smart enough to get on the train and come to the next stop, but they weren't, so we left the station and walked to their hood. We ran into Sabastian. I reached him before Ellie did, and I hooked off on him and decked him right in his jaw. Why didn't y'all come back? He went to speak, and I decked him again, this time harder than the first time. He said, please stop hitting me. It wasn't even my fault Amare's other girl got on the train, and he asked me to help him out, so of course I did. My heart was crushed. How could Amare have another girl? How could he love me and be with someone else? I was spiraling and, in an instant, enraged. And my petty is on one million in that very moment, I formulated a plan to fuck his friend Jimbo and hurt him just like he had hurt me. Play with my emotions. Are you dumb, stupid, crazy, or all of the above? Before I could put my plan into action, I would discover that I was, in fact, pregnant. I mean, we didn't use a condom, so what did I expect? But I had to exact my revenge before I could handle that issue, and so the unknown creature inside of me would have to wait.

Getting to Jimbo would be easy. He lived with Moe, so I called over there the next day and asked if Amare was there. He said no, cool, can I come over? He said yes. I made my way over to Moe's to link up with Jimbo. He buzzed me in, and when I walked into the apartment, he had the lights turned off, incense and candles burning, and slow music playing. I laughed to myself. I'm supposed to be seducing him, not the other way around. Anyway, the plan was to fuck him and bounce. I did just that, but the day I decided to enact my plan of revenge, one of his friends was there, and he went back and told Amare. I never fucked Jimbo after that, but the damage had been done. All this pain and heartache had accrued on the strength of a lie spun by Sabastian so he wouldn't get in trouble with Ellie. About four months after I had slept with Jimbo, Amare popped up at my grandmother's. Yup hadn't seen him in damn near half a year. I felt relieved I hadn't kept the baby, and I had wrestled with myself back and forth since I thought I was in love and the baby was made out of love. Why take its chance for greatness away? But my final decision was that I wasn't gonna be a single teenage momma, so I handled it.

Standing in front of her building, he looked broken and sad, and I was gloating and felt great about it. I walked over to him not with the same joy and happiness I had for over a year, but with an arrogance. However, I acted as if nothing happened and gave him a hug and a kiss. He barely spoke to me. We walked into the building and rode the elevator in silence. We sat in the staircase like we've done so many times before when I excused myself to go in and get my photo album cause we needed something to talk about. We had been sitting there in almost complete silence. He perked up a little, getting a glimpse into my life. He seemed as if he wanted to rewind time, running his fingers over pictures and asking questions. When he came across a picture of himself, Jimbo Sabastian and Moe. He took the picture from the album and crumbled it in his hand. He looked up at me with tears in his eyes and simply asked why. And I, with my current inflated ego, felt like I got him back for the hurt he caused me. I let loose all of what Sabastian told me and why I ended up breaking his heart. His next and last question was why I didn't speak to him, and my reasoning was simple. Your best friend asked me why he would lie to you. Then he told me the truth, and instantly I felt like shit. I felt so low that I started crying, pleading for him to forgive me. Amare simply held my face and told me he loved me and he would never stop loving me. It would be years before I would see Amare again. He and I have a story similar to that of Raymond; however, our story doesn't end; it's still ongoing, and for that, I'm eternally grateful. We are currently making new memories, and I can't say that this is it; however, I can say I'm enjoying the ride.

Now, during my period of "hoedom" and one of my breaks from Amare, one young man had me open, believing we were going to get married and have a wonderful life. Yes, he was a drug dealer and a wild African American, but so he dressed nicely, looked good, and had good hygiene. I have come across some nasty dudes with poor hygiene, and I just cannot do it. No, sir, I cannot deal with it. If you have a yuck mouth, got dirt under your nails, stank, or looked dirty, I cannot. Sidebar: I'm forever thankful and grateful not to have contracted anything during this period because I was reckless and clueless about the potential harm I might have brought to myself. Now, back to the guy who was already in his twenties, and I was barely sixteen. Chris, the color of cinnamon, tall, lanky, and bow-legged. He had the gift for gab and was a charmer, and that is exactly what he did: charmed me right out of my panties and into his bed. I could say he took advantage of me; however, I know right from wrong, and I knew sleeping with that grown-ass man was wrong and a mistake, but he made me feel loved, safe, wanted, and appreciated. He was the first guy to take me on a date to the movies and BBQ's boy, did I feel special; I felt like I finally had something and someone of my own. Chris made me feel appreciated. He checked in on me, made sure I ate daily, and after a few months of dating and fucking, you guessed it, he got me pregnant. I found out that I was pregnant randomly. I was on the train heading downtown when I got a sudden sharp pain in my lower right side. I thought it might have been my appendix, so I got off the train and went to the now-closed St. Vincent's Hospital, where they gave me an ultrasound and told me I had a large ovarian cyst that should go away; however, the pain that I felt was fetal movement. Fetal movement. Fluttering in my stomach, early movement of human life, how could I be pregnant? Damn, I went and made myself a damn hood rat project chick again. I kept this from everyone but God. I continued to date Chris and continued to live life as if I didn't know that I was pregnant. That is until I noticed my breasts getting larger. What pissed me off about him was that he knew I was pregnant. He never even asked me about being pregnant because he could see the changes in my body and mentioned that my breasts got bigger and, my hips seemed to have spread, and I hadn't had a period in a while. I figured this man that claimed he loved me and wanted to be with me would have made some kind of mention about the pregnancy, but he didn't just act like shit was the same. I just sucked it up and handled it like a champ. I mean, it's not like I hadn't done this before. I went into the phone book and found the number for an abortion clinic. Some of you may ask why I did this by myself, and the answer to that is that I have been in charge of myself since I was eight. I have always handled myself as an adult, and as an adult, I did adult things that had adult consequences. I had laid my fast tail down and gotten pregnant, so I would handle this by myself as well. The clinic I found was in Lower Pleasantville. This place had early morning and late-night hours.

And no, it was not a back alley or basement clinic, and this was back when girls who were close to 4 months could still have a two-day procedure and have a DuPont Induction-Evacuation. Or late-term abortion is where the clinician will place dilating sticks into your vagina to soften and open the cervix. The sticks are called laminaria sticks. Now, when I tell you this is painful, Lord Jesus, these hurts, but I couldn't be a certified ghetto statistic. I couldn't be a high school dropout with a baby on welfare, so I went through the procedure and went home. That night, Janet and Ralph were at my grandmother's, and although I was bent over in pain when they said we were going for a walk, I hopped on the chance to be in the cool night air. It felt good on my skin because, internally, I was burning up. The girls, Janet and Ralph, walked around Eagle Edge and Central Park for about an hour before returning upstairs to Lynn's. We did have school the next day. Only I was heading back to the clinic to have the second part of my abortion. So that morning, I showered, got dressed like always, and headed to the train. Now, this day, I ran into one of my classmates and I couldn't get off at the stop I needed to because she was expecting me to ride the train to the normal stop on the 14th and 7th. So, I did, but when getting off the train, I acted to get shoved back on the train so I could ride back uptown to 42nd and catch the shuttle. You are probably wondering how I was able to pay for this child. Medicaid is the absolute best insurance ever, and straight Medicaid, none of this health first or fidelity crap, just plain old Medicaid. I got to the clinic about forty-five minutes late, but they still saw me and asked if I had someone to take me home after, and I said yes. So, the nurse or tech, not sure as to what her title was, brought me into the back, where I changed into a gown and jumped up on the table. A large man walks in, and I think he is Russian. He said he was putting an IV in and that I'd be going to sleep. He put the IV in and pushed what looked like milk into my vein. I could feel the sting and warmth creep up my arm, and then my heart sped up, and then the techs were telling me I had to drink some apple juice and eat cookies before they could discharge me to my mother, and of course there was no parent once I felt good enough, I simply put on my clothes and left. This is one of the reasons why I say God is good. After a two-day procedure, you are supposed to be on antibiotics, but being that I had no adult coming to get me, I just bounced. No infection, no fever, nothing. It was great. After the abortion, I continued to date Chris for about a month, but since I couldn't have sex, he ended up ghosting me, which is fine because he didn't like wearing condoms, and I didn't want to get pregnant again. Which I would, but not by Chris, by a hood Wild African American named Jordan, and then, of course, by my ex-husband, one miscarriage, and my one and only heartbeat Legend.

Living in Eagle Edge, I got to have a semi-normal teenage life. I always had a boyfriend, mostly because my cousin had one, and would hook me up with one of their friends or a random cousin. We would explore the outside world, play games like manhunt, red light-green light, ding-dong ditch, or just find all the secret paths in Central and Riverside Parks. The girls and I had different cliques that went along with our different stages in life. During one of those stages, I would meet Noah. At the time, we didn't know he was younger than us. He lied so that he could hang out with us. You know he wanted to kick it with the big dogs! Noah was a cute kind of short dark-skinned kid with braces and glasses. What he lacked in height, he made up with his personality cause the kid was funny as hell. I would have loved to have been his girlfriend. However, he would end up dating Ellie. As he claims, he feared my cousin, and she forced him to date her. Either way, we remained friends throughout the years but seriously reconnected later as adults. Damn social media. We started chatting through social media and then started to hang out. Unfortunately for me, Noah was in a very complicated situation, well, shit in three complex situations. He had a pending court case looming over his head, was married, and had a baby from a woman with whom he was engaged. Crazy, right? Well, my stupid ass went headfirst into a semi-relationship, knowing all this just because of our past acquittance. I thought I'd get treated a little differently because of that. So, I started falling for him and opening up to him.

I allowed him to claim a part of my heart. Dumb cause most nights I was laying in my bed lonely, wanting to roll over and just have him hold me or kiss my forehead, but he was home with his fiancée and kid. I let him play in my face and with my feelings for about two years, and then I had to do like Ashanti and become unfoolish. I blocked him on all platforms until I could be around him without lusting after him. I had to detox him out of my system. I don't know what it is about bad boys and Wild African Americans, but they just do it for me.

While living at Lynns's, a homeless transgender woman named Tonya would become my best friend in Eagle Edge. She would steal me a fifth of rum almost every day after school and sometimes on the weekends, and all I had to do was give her two dollars. Of course, Tonya was a crackhead and had no moral compass. So, she went to the liquor store, and the two dollars would be hers. This ill-fated toxic friendship is why I would have to go to summer school in order to graduate in August 1997. I would become a functional alcoholic, masking my feelings of hurt and pain with liquor so I could mustard up a fake smile throughout the day, self-medicating myself with drinks so I didn't have to deal with my reality. In the liquor-infused daze I was existing, my grades no longer mattered, my siblings no longer mattered, and I no longer mattered. But in the fall of 1997, I would meet someone who would spark a match inside of me and want me to succeed and be happy with myself.

Now, I graduated from HPHS in August 1997, when I was seventeen. During the Fall of 1997, I would turn eighteen, and I would meet the young man of my dreams, Raymond. We would meet at a party on the hill (St. Gwen Terrace). Now, Raymond is two years younger than me, but that made no difference to me. He was tall chocolate with a red undertone to his skin. He had the most beautiful smile I had ever seen and soulful deep brown eyes that, when I looked at them, I could see my future. Or, at the very least, a version of a future that looked like peace.

Raymond, being the fly-handsome guy he was, would break my heart a few times, not that he was trying to; we were both young and if we met later in life, things would have been different. Now, Raymond and I share a few things in common. One was our parents' drug addiction. The second was being the eldest child. Third was that we lived with our grandparents, and finally, we just wanted so much more from life than what we were given.

He would be the second guy I'd let completely into my world. I would sit on his couch and tell him my whole life story. We connected on a different level. The energy, or whatever you want to call it, between us was electrifying. Raymond would end up being the first guy that I would give head to, and I was allegedly the first he went down on. I must say he did it too good for it to have been his first time. We laugh about that because he swears it was his first time. Using a large peppermint ball in his mouth. It was a warm and cold sensation all at once; he should trademark that. During one of our breakups, while he was in school out in Toronto, I flew out there to spend a few days with him. It was the first time we had spent more than a day together, the first sleepover we would have, and boy, did we make good use of that time. Shoot, we even broke a bed. Well, it was a futon, but we still broke it and had an amazing time doing so. Raymond and I would be dating other people, but we would always link back up no matter who we were with until he finally became serious about the woman who would become his wife. It does make me wonder, but I won't dwell on it, so now it is purely a friendship between him and me. I'm ok with that. I love black love, and I want

Raymond to be happy, healthy, and loved. He seems to be all of the above. Raymond will always hold a special place in my heart.

One random Sunday, I would be visiting my aunt, Janet, having a grand old time like normal: good food, laughs and excellent company. Heading back to Lynns's, one of my uncle Ralphs's nephews was on the corner of 116th with Jordan. I stopped to speak to Stanley and shot the breeze for a minute. We played C-low. I cleaned them out and headed down the block when Stanely called my name.

I stopped and turned around and saw Jordan running up the block. Jordan, this thin yet muscular chocolate of a man with kissable lips and dark brown eyes the color of cherry red oak, and of course with him being in front of me showing me any kind of interest had me at a loss for words for a hot second and then as I thought I was spitting game to this obvious player. But staring into Jordan's eyes, I just knew I could trust him, and maybe if I was grown and lived on my own, I could have, but being 17, I was still living with Lynn. So, the conversation we had basically went like this: "Yo shorty, I think you're kinda fly. Are you single?" Even if I wasn't single, I was going to tell him I was, but fortunately, I was very single, so I giggled and said yes. He gave me his number, and I gave him Lynn's number because I didn't have a pager, and cell phones weren't a thing yet.

Jordan ended up walking me all the way home, and we chatted about nothing and everything. He held my hand as he walked me home, and the warmth in his hand seemed to circulate through his body and into mine.

We made it to the front of my building, and as I hugged him, he bent down and kissed me with his pillow lips, and I melted. I literally floated upstairs. I don't even think I took the elevator and glided up all 12 flights. Jordan and I never exactly went out on any dates, but we would watch TV and cuddle at his house. On about the 5th cuddle date, his hands started to roam over my body, lingering at intimate parts and flicking my nipple between his thumb and forefinger while gently kissing the nape of my neck. With each touch, I grew hotter. With each kiss, I grew wetter. His hand started to explore my thighs and inner thighs, sliding into my ugly green panties. I jumped when his fingers touched my second set of lips and quivered as he inserted two fingers and started to move them in and out of me. Small, hot moans escaped from my now dry mouth from all of my panting. And then, in one swift move, he turned me around, propped me up on all fours, and kissed my back while he continued to finger me. I could feel a pressure building up inside of me like a balloon ready to pop when his mouth engulfed my mound of wetness, and I exploded in his mouth. He told me I tasted like honey, which is where the name 'honeepot' came from. As I lay on my stomach, he was fumbling for a condom. I saw it in his hand. I saw him open the package, but I didn't watch to see if he put it on, and as his body sensually crashed into mine from the back, he let go of all his essence unbeknownst to me, and he would be my second baby daddy.

When I found out I was pregnant, I confronted him, and of course, he apologized and explained that the condom had popped right as he was about to climax. I didn't see the condom; however, I saw him act as if he was taking something off and disposing of it. Did Jordan tell me the truth; who's to know? I do know I ended up getting an abortion for a second time, and my self-worth hit an all-time low.

My father's side of the family used to have yearly BBQs called 'Friends and Family.' Sometimes, we were in Morningside Park, and sometimes, we were in Jefferson Park, but it was always toward the end of the summer, like a last hooray before school started. At one of these 'Friends and Families,' I would meet Mel. Even though I knew Mel before 'Friends and Family,' he claims to have only met me there. So, I'll go with his lead.

In the summer of 2004, Mel and I met in Jefferson Park at Friends and Family. He was visiting his family; he had moved to Baton Rouge and would come back to New Brunswick from time to time. So, let's set the mood: it is a hot and hazy, overcast day at the end of August, with people all over the park having their own cookouts and just mingling, enjoying the last days of summer. I was standing by the gate, wearing a red, black, and white tube top with jean-like capris. He had on baggy jean shorts and a yellow shirt.

Oh, Mel is the only male I have ever talked to, dated, and had sex with who is shorter than me, but the energy he gives off is that of a man who is six feet tall, and he is as handsome as all outdoors. Now that I've gotten that off my chest, I caught him staring at me, and I thought to myself, he's handsome, but his older sister is my hood aunt, so that kind of makes him my hood uncle. But fuck it, we're not blood. Don't judge me; we wouldn't have sex until years later in the 2020s. When we made eye contact, sparks flew. Who knew you could fall into lust at first sight? Mel walked up to me after getting the scoop from his sister and started talking to me. Normally, I'm not the friendliest person, but there was something about him that put me at ease, and we hit it off. And yes, I know you're saying, "Damn, bitch, every dude you link with, you fall in love with," and the answer is no. I have been in love with five men and one woman. Again, I have been with a lot of people, and maybe it wasn't love that I was in, but I digress.

Mel and I walked around that park for hours, holding hands, talking, and just gazing into each other's eyes. I know that sounds corny, but it is the truth. We didn't even kiss until years later. Mel just felt like he was the missing part of my soul that I didn't even know I had lost. He knew my inner thoughts and what made me tick. Mel got me like no other. So, when I have problems with men or women, I call him to vent and get a male perspective. Mel is one of the five men I have fallen in love with and will always love, no matter what. But Mel is married. He is another man in my life who is in the wrong time and the wrong place. Like most relationships, we have had ups and downs. We've gone from not talking to not seeing each other, but no matter what, we always find our way back to each other. Shit, I would even tell Mel to leave me alone, and he'd give me a break sometimes for a few years. But he is my rock, my reasoning when I'm in doubt or feel like I'm losing myself. He is always there for me.

For lack of better terms, I'm the female version of Mel on an emotional level. Okay, okay, y'all little nasties, y'all wanna know how he laid it down, right? Well, I did say he was in the top five. I will not say where he landed, but he was the closest ever to making me tap out. He left me weak in the knees and out of breath. I hope that answers your question. Oh, I will say Mel is the most romantic and respectful of me. He handles me with such tenderness, yet he has dominance over me, and I completely become submissive to him. Maybe it's because we built this amazing friendship over the past twenty years, or maybe it's the fact that he has love and respect for me. Either way, Mel—just wow, Mel. Nah, it was just amazing fucking sex, nothing more, nothing less. I said I was a hoe, lol. Now, let's move on.

CHAPTER 8: JAMES'S DEATH

The death of James came as no surprise to me. He had lung cancer that had spread throughout his body, and he didn't care too much about his health or getting treatment. He slowly and painfully withered away and died. The last time I saw James alive, he was living at his mother's house and was skeletal. James always had a big head, but now he looked like a bobblehead before those things even became popular. He was sad and pleasant, even soft-spoken. He called me 'Poopscoop,' and I hated that name. Why give someone the nickname of something used to pick up dog shit? Is that how he viewed me because I wasn't his kid? I don't know. I do know it made my teeth grind every time he called me that.

"I'm sorry," James said, and at that moment, all the hate I had for him had left my body. It was like I was looking at a helpless child that realized they had been doing something fucked up and got caught, so how then could I hold on to the hate I had when this man was dying and trying to make amends for all his wrongdoings. I thought about the times we went camping and how he showed me the best place to put the chicken thigh in the cage so we could catch the most crabs, and I felt sad. I felt cheated that I didn't have more good memories of this man who was such a major part of my life. So, I said, "I know James," and I placed my hand on top of his shoulder. I felt the smooth roundness of his shoulder bone and wonder if he would hold on much longer, but if he didn't, I hoped my action had absolved him of all his sins and the role he played in my miserable childhood. I hoped that eased his conscience enough that it no longer felt like a weight on his chest. He said it again: "Poopscoop, I'm sorry." This time, I was looking directly into his face, and I could tell he meant it. So, I told him I forgave him and that it was ok. I said, "Get some rest, and I'll see you later," as I got up to walk out of the room. He said, "Goodbye, Poopscoop," and I waved goodbye. I walked back up front with his mom and chatted for a few more minutes before I left to go home. That was the last time I ever saw my stepfather alive.

This was the very first time I ever looked at him as my stepfather, and that saddened me. The next time I saw him was in his casket. Gathered in the funeral home were his mother, his living siblings, his children, his ex-wife, and my mother, his life partner. The ending of his life was the beginning of my mother's rebirth into the single world, but she really hadn't changed. She still would become lost in every man she would deal with, leaving me to come and regulate like I was the commander in charge. Honestly, I was the commander in charge. That's always been my position. The thing is, I didn't want the position anymore. In fact, I never did it was forced on me. And I handled it like I've handled everything in life like a fucking G! When shit gets rough or raggedy, Amber calls, and I come and get shit right again, but I'm tired. I think I'll finally let her be the mom from now on.

CHAPTER 9: BOLD PROGRAM

Getting back on track, I'm a high school graduate, a feat that neither of my parents carried out well. My dad would get his GED in prison, but like I was saying, I completed the first task of becoming an adult Monique. By the time I finished twelfth grade, my GPA was in the toilet, so I only got accepted into Dax Community College into the nursing program. The only problem there was that the program had a five-year waiting list, so after two semesters, I left and enrolled in a school called CTI (Caliber Training Institute). There, I would become a medical assistant, and, in my head, I felt like this was the best that I could do for a young girl of eighteen/nineteen. It was decent money, the hours were good, and I got to vacation. But I wouldn't put that skill set to use until later on. I started working at Bold Program. Actually, Ellie got me the job there since she had already been working there for about two years. I had two positions there before I went on to be a Medical Assistant. My first position at Bold was as a childcare worker. I worked in the red room with the kindergarteners and first graders.

In this room, I would meet my Caramel Flan spitfire best friend, Chole. She is younger than me but also has had so much responsibility placed on her from a young age that she gives off the appearance that she is older and much more mature. Now, when I say she is a spitfire, I mean her temper, her fuse, whatever you want to call it, is short, which is why she is quiet and mainly keeps to herself. We instantly clicked and have been rocking with each other ever since. We both quickly rose through the ranks and ended up in the office as assistant managers. The only difference is that I also had pay roll in my task of things to do. Now, here in the office, I would meet the kindest, sweetest person to ever share space with, my French Vanilla best friend Stacey. She operated the teen lounger and leadership programs for young adults from the ages of thirteen to eighteen. This was a stipend program to keep the kids off the streets and out of trouble. Now, Chole, Stacey, and I will eventually just be running the office by ourselves. The higher-ups would check in occasionally to show face, especially for the Saturday morning academy. When we spent money, we needed one of them to sign off on what we wanted to get, and the receipts had to account for every penny spent. You see, Bold was a not-for-profit organization, so they had to show proof of how they were spending the granted money they received. Now, on those Saturday mornings, we all would stroll in light from the Friday night. Breakfast always consisted of either a bagel with cream cheese and bacon or a bacon egg and cheese with a Pepsi coffee or tea. Those poor kids, we were such shifty counselors, but we made it work, and our kids would go on to be college graduates. Something one could be proud of is that we contributed to their process and helped them not to become statistics but to make new statistics of poor children living in low economic status. As for us, we still were growing and learning as well, and being that our role models were ourselves because the adults in our lives were more fucked up than us, what did we have to go off. If you ask me, we did alright.

Shoot, let me tell you how Stacey, Chole, and I almost got kidnapped at the end of every summer the Bold program had a Unity March. Chole, Stacey, and I, as usual, were late and trying to make it to the train. There was a cute guy on the corner who asked if we needed a ride. Of course, we all said yeah. The funny thing is we all were thinking if Homeboy tried anything, he was gonna get his ass whooped. Anyway, we gave him the destination, and we sat in the back talking amongst ourselves when Chole said, "Yo, where is you going?" Homie said, "Oh, you girls looked like you wanted to have some fun," and before I knew what was happening, my French Vanilla Stacey had him in a headlock and was like pull this car over right now. Chole pulled out her pocket knife and pressed it into his side, so you know I couldn't just sit there and let them have all the fun. I had to get my lick in, so I pulled out my keys that had the master lock attached and clocked him in his head a couple of times with the lock, and he started leaking and almost crashed. Sisters linked in insanity cause we could've died. We all coursed his ass out, and, of course, he obliged, pulled over, and we jumped out. He sped off as soon as our feet hit the pavement. Oh well, he should have done better with his decision-making. We were like ten blocks past the start of the march, so we just hoofed it back down. But honestly, what he thought was gonna happen was like you picked the wrong ones for any foolishness that day, homie. We laughed and chatted about the bullshit that had just happened as we continued our walk to the march. That was Chole and mine first and only time attending the march. I love these girls. They are my sisters. Shit, they are my son's Godmothers. I trust them with mine and his life. And visa versa.

During my time at Bold, I would meet my son's father and my husband, Sam Crawford Jr. Of course, one of my cousins hooked us up. Michi was dating his cousin, Richard. Michi and Richard had a turbulent relationship that would end with them having deep admiration, respect and love for each other, which made them close friends. I won't go into detail about them; I just know it was rough and loving all at once. And I'll be getting back to Sam in a minute.

CHAPTER 10: AUNT CRYSTAL

My aunt Crystal is Amber's baby sister and the youngest of her siblings. She has three daughters and one son. Amber's kids and her kids are roughly around the same age. So Crystal was the cool aunt on my mother's side. We loved going over to her house and chilling with our cousins, but then we moved back to New Brunswick. Crystal was a CNA-certified nursing assistant. She drove and had her own place and money. She and her husband, Griz, went to a party, and something happened to her. She lost her mind. I think someone spiked her drink, but I wasn't there, and besides, who am I to be making diagnosis? When Crystal lost her way, Griz secretly divorced her and remarried a chick he had been cheating on her with. Kicked her out of the house they shared and disregarded her like trash. I swear some men aint 't shit. Crystal, now homeless, would start hopping from one friend's house to another, and on one alleged drug-fueled night, Crystal had ice-picked a man to death. She had spent some time in a mental institute. Apparently, she has a dissociative personality disorder, and she herself wasn't the murderer, but one of her personalities I know sounds made up, but trust me, it's God's honest truth.

Anyway, the hospital released her to the care of Amber when they felt she was well enough to be discharged, which is approximately a year after she killed someone. My mother decided to assign me the responsibility of getting Crystal to all her appointments while living with her. The first task was the Social Security office here. I saw the extent of her fractured mind. Or the very Oscar-worthy act she put on. Crystal jumped up at every number that was called, and I mean every number. She got up and tried to walk to the front, and every time she got out of her seat, I grabbed her hand and gently sat her down and told her that it was not her turn, and her number was 87A. And while I sat here and babysat my overgrown adult aunt, I wondered how I had gotten bamboozled into this. Having to stop her from fighting two different times and praying that her number would be called soon, I was over-sitting there, beyond annoyed. The first fight was because she thought the lady beside her was trying to steal her shoes. Yes, I know her shoes; however, this lady had bent down to tie her own shoes and Crystal thought she tried to take her shoes.

So I quickly defused that by telling the lady my aunt had not taken her medication. The second fight I walked back in on, I got up to use the bathroom briefly, and Crystal was in this lady's face and cursing her out. The lady pushed Crystal, and Crystal grabbed this lady and tried to ram her head into the ground. At the very same time I reached them, Crystal's number had finally been called, and I pulled Crystal off of her and pushed her toward the front. Hey, this is your number. They finally called you to let go. I got her to the front, apologized to the woman she was fighting with, and sat down to wait for her to be finished in the back and get her back to my mom's. This experience was traumatic, and I was tired. When I heard my name being called over the loudspeaker. I walked back up to the front, gave them my name, and I'm told them to come around to the back, where Aunt Crystal was sitting at a desk with a portly middle-aged case worker. She had on a plaid jumpsuit with large box braids that needed to come out over three weeks ago, which she paired with tacky patent leather shoe boots where you could see the leather pulling away from the shoe. So, I walked over there and asked what was going on, and the case worker said I need you to translate for me.

Confused, I asked her what she was talking about, and she spoke English. I turned to Aunt Crystal and asked what she was talking about. Crystal said niecey, I do not know so I turned back to the case worker and asked what she asked her, and she said her full name. Baffled and upset, I turned back to Crystal and said your name? Come on, Crystal, your name, she said, niecey. I told this dizzy bitch my name. What else does she need to know? So, I told the case worker her name, address, and date of birth, all while Crystal was sitting there talking to herself well, cursing the worker out. However, the worker was doing her best and was being professional. She then tells me that she isn't supposed to do this but lets me know that my aunt is approved, and she will be getting not one but two checks. She will be getting her acceptance letter in the mail shortly. Great, awesome, let's get the hell out of here. I took Aunt Crystal back to my mother's and unloaded on my mother. I had told her that I could not continue to take care of her sister it was driving me crazy. She agreed to take on more of her sisters' responsibilities, which was fine with me. I called my grandmother and told her I was staying the night with my mother only so she would not be worried. Now, my mother worked the mid-shift from 3-11, so my sister, brothers, Aunt Crystal, and I were in the house. Around nine that night, Aunt Crystal walked out of the front door wearing only a nightgown and socks. I walked out behind her, calling her name, but she never responded to me as she walked into the staircase.

I walked back into the apartment and locked the door. Joy asked me where Aunt Crystal had gone. Did she have her keys? My reply to both was I do not know. I locked the door, and after straightening up, I went to bed. My mother and her then-boyfriend Clyde came home around 1 am. I heard them when they came in, so I got up and greeted them in the front. She was making Dinty more beef stew. I asked if I could have some, and she said sure, just clean up after yourself. Cool, before they went into the back, she asked me where my aunt was, and I told her the story of her leaving in her socks and nightgown. She said cool and went to bed. I finished my stew and climbed back into the bed with Joy. As soon as I lay down, Joy whispered in my ear that she was under the bed. Not too sure as to what she said, I said what in an elevated voice, and she hushed me and, in a voice a little above a whisper, said that she was under the bed and she was scared. With that information, I had to see if she was telling the truth, so I rolled over her and looked under the bed, and as sure as the sky appeared blue in the morning. Aunt Crystal was under the bed, and she was smoking a cigarette. I rolled back over and said oh shit, now I'm scared. I tell Joy I'm going to get mommy, and she says please. I start counting to three so I can gas myself up, jump off the bed, and dash to my mother's room. As I'm banging on the door, it swings open, and as she closes her robe, she asks, "What is the problem" and I tell her about her sister being under the bed smoking and scaring us. Now, you are going to think this is a joke, but my mother bent down and asked her sister what she was doing under the bed, and she replied that it was safe. My mother said safe from who, and Crystal said you know Amber, it's safe from them.

My mother then gathered all the kids and assembled us into her room, so we all piled into her small, cramped room: myself, Joy, Jet, Jim, and Clyde. Later that morning, we were all up watching Saturday morning cartoons, and I smelled gas, but I have a nose like a bloodhound. I kept asking if anyone else could smell it, but I was the only one, so my mother told me to check it out. Now, remember Aunt Crystal was still out there, so I snook out of my mother's room and walked down the hall to discover Aunt Crystal trying to blow us up. She blew out the gas plight on the stove and oven. She had placed paint and roach cans in the oven and was trying to ignite them with us all in the house. I ran back into my mother's room and told her what she was doing. Now, this Saturday would be the first time I would see my mother fight and be scared for the other person she was fighting. She was beating the breaks off of Aunt Crystal. So I slid in between the two of them. As I did that, Crystal reached around me and snatched some of my mother's locs out of her head, and at that very moment, she knocked me down and started to choke her. After all the commotion, Clyde finally came out of the room, pulled my mother into the room, peeked his head out, and said, get Crystal out of here. That's what Joy and I did: gathered her up and a few small bags and took her to the port authority. The train ride there was quite strangely peaceful after all that had happened. Aunt Crystal broke the silence and said she was sorry and that she really loved us. Joy asked her what the hell was that. How could you do that to us? She mumbled something under her breath and started crying. She broke down and told us how much she loved us again and how she never wanted to hurt us, how she was trying to control them, but sometimes they pushed her to the side, and she was not able to regain control until it was too late. And truth be told, this was way too late for her to try to fix. My mother would never let her sister live with her again. And even though we had no clue where she would end up, we told her to keep in touch. Crystal promised us she would, kissed us, and then walked into the bus depot. This would not be the last time we saw Aunt Crystal or be involved in her shenanigans.

Chapter 11: Ellie and Michi

I would have many adventures with my cousins. They helped shape me into the person I currently am I was very standoffish and scared of my own voice. From them, I learned that it is okay to be pretty and tough. I learned the meaning of true loyalty when I say they had and still have my back. They most definitely had my back. And if one got in trouble, we all got in trouble, and most of our trouble was breaking curfew. Time isn't a concept for kids having fun in the summer, winter, spring, or fall. We were just out having a ball, and that street light rule didn't apply to us. Summertime, however, was the best time. There was the pool directly across the street from our building, which we usually climbed over the gate and went to the night pool, walked to the 110th Street pool, stopping at the Chinese restaurant to get six chicken wings chopped up with mad salt pepper hot sauce and ketchup with an order of fries or Tostones that we shared between the three of us. One particular day we decided that we wanted to go to Bloomfield Island and which was a long ass ride from 103rd Street to that last stop on the D train.

On this day, we also recruited our friend who lived in the building with us. Mindy is Puerto Rican and Irish, I know. It's a weird combo; however, Mindy was the sweetest girl with the filthiest mouth I have ever heard. Here I think I curse like a sailor nah, Mindy invented all the curse words in the book. So, the four of us walk from Amsterdam Avenue to Central Park to get the train and take this long ass ride into Puerto Plato. We clowned around on the train doing front and back flips off the poles shit. I couldn't do that now if I tried. This old body does not bounce like it used to. Anyway, I'm sure we annoyed everyone in the cart we were in, but we were young and living life, so fuck them and however they felt. We finally made it to Bloomfield Island and thank goodness, because we had started getting sleepy and didn't want to take the chance of falling asleep and the train making its way back to Canton.

Running wild in Puerto Plato, and the first ride we got on was the hell hole. They eventually shut this ride down, however shit. This ride fucked us up and had us dizzy and nauseous at the same time. My neck and head hurt. Ellie was limping, and Michi and Mindy were holding each other up. After about half an hour, we composed ourselves and were able to continue with the rest of the day. We had enough money for about three more rides, something to eat, and a few games. While we were playing games, a group of kids that I assume were from that area bumped Mindy and knocked her down. Not knowing Mindy was with us, we helped her and asked them if there was a problem.

Well, Ellie did since she was tougher and had less fear than the rest of us. Ellie was like the enforcer in the group. The biggest girl in that group said, Yeah and before she could finish her sentence, Ellie, being Ellie, swung on that girl and knocked out her front tooth. In what seemed like unison, we all said damn and held our faces, and then streets next to the Cyclone erupted into a may lay. I had never seen Mindy get down, but she was with all the smoke, throwing hands, kicking, and biting. I was more shocked to see her fighting than I was to be involved in the fight. We carried on for what seemed like forever, but some of the attendants from the rides broke us up and kept the group from Puerto Plato with them as we walked off in opposite directions, but boy was, we hyped adrenal pumping through us we were on demon time at this point even Mindy who was the timid one out of all. We dared anyone to try us at this point as we walked back to the train for that long ride back to Canton. And on that train, still buzzing from the day's adventure, we just laughed as we replayed the whole day over and over, and of course, you know we were late getting back home, so Lynn put us on punishment. Mindy was lucky her parents were asleep when she got upstairs, so there was no punishment for her breaking curfew. It didn't matter much; she sometimes sat in the hallway with us. That excitement would last us for a while as we constantly talked about the events of that day until the next adventure occurred and would now be the new highlight. While living at Lynn's, she constantly went down south, leaving my cousins and me home alone for weeks, so we made the best of what we could. There is a church right across the street from Lynn's building, and we attended this church fairly often. They served juice, coffee, and crackers right before service. This church was a very large church with secret rooms. When we got bored, we would wander around the church, playing games, sitting in the rafters, and watching. On one of Lynn's many trips down south, she left us with one hundred dollars to take care of three teenage girls for three weeks. So, we improvised and decided to rummage through the coat room and in the pockets of the people downstairs, hearing the word of God. We chalked this up to God's understanding that we had been starving, so that outweighed the sin of stealing because of what God would want or let children starve. Now, this would not be our only time robbing the church. We would rob the church's congregants approximately three more times. On the fourth time we did this, the church announced for everyone to hold onto their wallets and change purses. So, our plight as the Robin Hoods of the hood and church came to a crashing end, but by this time, Lynn had returned, and we returned to our normal way of life of torture and cold existence under Lynn's care.

Much of my favorite memories of living at Lynn's come from spending time with Ellie and Michi, and I thank them for loving me and helping me bring the more urban side of me out. My cousins have taught me how to keep a song in my heart and a bounce in my step. They showed me that I could be girly and a tomboy all at the same time. They showed me that living life is meant to be lived. Yes, we have responsibilities; however, we have a responsibility to ourselves, and they helped me see that. We are still very close. However, we are not as close as we were as children. Nonetheless, those are my girls, and living with them provided me with access to actually living, so to them, I'm eternally grateful.

CHAPTER 12: SAM

Now, back to our regular programming. Dating Sam was like a ride at the amusement park. What an adrenaline rush I got every time I was with him. He took me places I had never been, treated me like I was special, and meant something to him. Tall, light-skinned, and handsome with light brown eyes, Sam was my knight in shining armor, but we would betray each other and break the trust we once had. It's safe to say he was looking for someone to be a yes sir and jump when asked to jump, and baby, that has never been me. For me, he was a bit of a square. He lacked that bad boy edge I liked so much, and it's not like I hadn't fallen in love with him, but the only love I knew how to give and receive was toxic. I should have known that he was trouble—most light-skinned people are devil-sent. I know, I know, I'm a colorist, but this is my opinion, and my feelings are valid. Unfortunately, there is so much bad history here in our story that I could actually write a book just based on that. However, out of that history, we got married and had the most perfect baby boy ever.

Getting to have our son—Lord God, was almost impossible. We would break up so many times. I would move out and get my own place, then move back in again. I would change the locks. Yes, I can change the locks; I told you I'm rough around the edges. But from the age of eighteen to thirty-two, we were together through his cheating, my cheating, his immaturity, and my lack of patience. To be fair to him, I didn't know how to be a wife; I never saw one in real life from my immediate side of the family. He didn't know how to be a husband; his parents divorced at an early age. So, instead of a husband, I got an extra child, and instead of him getting a wife, he got a cold, distant roommate. Do you know what it's like living with a spoiled grown man-child? It's exhausting. He couldn't function on his own—well, at least that's the façade he put on when we moved in together. Him always comparing me to his mother or his grandmothers drove me crazy. What grown man still has his grandma cutting his steak for him? I mean, come on. I think no, I know I stayed with Sam well past the expiration date of that relationship because he chose me. And that's all I wanted was to feel wanted to feel seen, to feel like someone didn't see me as an option but as the main prize.

In the meantime, I enrolled, started, and completed training at CTI to become a Medical Assistant. Sam and I moved in together because my grandma kicked me out, which I guess turned out to be a blessing in disguise. Sam was instrumental in me getting back into college and finishing what I started. He was right by my side, and for that, I'm grateful. Don't get me wrong, it wasn't all grim and depressing in the marriage. It's just that it got stale, and no one bothered to try and refresh it and make it work. Sam would say to me, "Monique, you're too smart. Don't settle for being a Medical Assistant. Work hard, and you can be more." His father had played for the New Brunswick Knights, a bum-ass team that has not won the NBA Championship since 1973, and then became a high school basketball coach, so I guess this was his pep talk as he says he saw potential in me. I guess that little fact about his life made him an aficionado.

Anyway, Sam made me realize that I was more than a Medical Assistant, and if I were determined to break these generational curses that had been plaguing my family, I'd have to put on my big girl panties, buckle down, and take care of business. Any challenge or obstacle I would overcome would blossom, grow, and be great. So, I enrolled in Joan of Arc Community College in January 2003 and picked up where I left off in Dax.

While Sam and I were together, I would pick up the boys—my boys—for the weekends and take them to the movies or just to get away from home. I felt like they needed some peace since their father had died, and our mother, now mostly clean, was still unintentionally neglectful of people's feelings. I guess it was me trying to keep them close and make sure they felt loved. I wanted them to feel chosen and wanted, just like I had longed for it in my youth. I felt like they longed for it, too. My life is so closely entwined with my siblings at this point it seemed like my life merged into theirs. At this point, she was feeling herself a little more and wanted to be around her peers, so hanging with her big sister, and I was cool with that. I still checked in her to make sure she was safe.

Sidebar: Oh, how could I leave out the baby of the bunch? On June 23rd, 2004, my father had his last child. I know he's an old man, and I'm his eldest and will already be 25 years older than Riley. Riley is her name cute, right? However, I felt more like come on pops, keep that thing wrapped up. You're too old to be having babies. However, my youngest sister is the funniest little girl I've ever met and is still the sweetest girl/young lady I know. When Riley was born, she looked like a baby glow worm. You know, one of those toys from the 80s, their cheeks light up and fill the room with warmth when you squeeze it. That's my Riley, filling every room with warmth and love. Overly protective of our father, she really thought he was hers alone, and she and I would argue she didn't understand the concept of him having children outside of her mother for a few years. She eventually got it and learned to share Kevin with all of his children. Once I had Legend, she and he would become inseparable. They are more like brother and sister, but she takes being an aunt seriously while Legend pays her no mind. I'm happy they get along and have each other to lean on. Having someone that can relate to you is a blessing.

During my last semester at Joan of Arc Community College, Sam and I were just about done in a relationship that was taking us nowhere. We would have a night of drunken sex, but not that drunk because we used a condom. I told you we both were cheating. The condom would break, and that morning, I would wake him up to take me to the clinic to get the morning-after pill. At that time, you needed a prescription. I took it as directed, and my period came.

Thank you, God, I dodged a bullet. Ok, so last semester, all bets were off. I got to come out the gate strong. The last semester is stressful. I could not afford to fail. I have a lot riding on my back, so many people are looking up to me at this point. I will be the first person from my mom and my father's side to have this small piece of paper that does not mean much, but it signifies that my family can succeed. We don't all have to be welfare recipients, and in section 8, we can and will be more. Meanwhile, I'm losing weight, which I attribute to stress. I have no appetite, which I also blame on stress, but now there is this nasty metallic taste in my mouth almost like I have been chewing on pennies. Sam takes notice of the weight loss and says maybe you're pregnant. This pissed me off because I'm like, didn't you take me to get the morning-after pill, and have I not been having periods? Duh, don't be trying to piss me off for no reason.

But something must be wrong with me, Lord. I'm dying, aren't I, Lord? Not now. I have come so far and have so much more to do. Yes, all that was in my head, I was panicking. I said it must be a tumor; I couldn't be pregnant. I have my period right now, which I did. He said I should take a test anyway. I told him, "No, I'm not wasting money on something that I know I'm not." The next night, I came in from work and class, and there was Sam with a pregnancy test. He said just take it and humor me. Cool. Whatever, I'll do it. I head to the bathroom to pee on the stick and take a shower. I take my clothes off, sit on the toilet, and pee on the stick. I set it on top of the toilet and got in the shower. I always play music when in the shower, so I let two songs play and peeked out behind the shower curtain. I passed out and hit the ground.

I do not know if Sam heard me fall or was just coming into the bathroom to use it, but I know when I came to, I was in his arms, and he was holding the stick. I looked down at his hand, and there it was in bright pink two solid lines. I started crying because I was in a state of disbelief. This just could not be life right now; I was so close to getting away and out of this relationship. So close, but no cigar. I got up, dried off, and put my clothes on because I needed to go to the drugstore. Sam is an idiot, and he must have picked up the wrong type of test. There are three pharmacies in the area that Sam and I live in, and I brought tests from all three and all three tests came back positive, and it feels like all the wind had been knocked out of my lungs. Sam's next question was, "What are we going to do?" And I said there is no 'we' in this. I'm getting rid of this, so that next morning, I made an appointment to go to the "chop shop" abortion clinic. The following morning, I had such a terrible headache, and I felt dizzy, I guess because I had not eaten since the night before. You must stop eating at least eight hours before the procedure. When I arrived at the clinic, I checked in and took a seat.

The tech calls my name, and I'm taken into the back, and blood work and a sonogram are done. After the blood work and sonogram were done, I was seated in a room, but the tech didn't give me a bag to place my items in or a gown to change into. She tells me to sit and wait. I'm sitting in the room waiting for someone to come in and put this IV in, take my belongings, and give me a gown so we can get this over and done with, and finally, in walks the tech and Dr. Miller. He says, "Ms. Mitchell Side bar (I never use my married last name). We are unable to provide you with the services you request," and why not? I screamed, feeling like they singled me out to destroy my life. Dr. Miller says that I'm eighteen weeks pregnant, so I laugh and say oh, that's the issue. I'm ok with the two-day process. Dr. Miller sits next to me, places his hand on my shoulder, and says you are having this baby; the laws have changed, and there are no more two-day procedures unless your life is in danger from the pregnancy, and yours is not. There was a small window in the room, and I stared out of the window, having just one thought. TRAPPED. I'm TRAPPED. I cannot breathe. My head is spinning. I need water, I need help, I need Jesus. A single tear drops from my right eye.

Dr. Miller saw the panic and discomfort in my face and asked me if I was ok. I said yes and continued to look out the window. What am I going to do with a baby from a man that I don't love anymore or want to be with? This right here is a disaster. I sat there and cried for about twenty minutes before I was able to pull myself together, and just before I was about to leave, a social worker came in and said Dr. Miller sent her to talk to me. I didn't want to talk to anyone; all I wanted to do was run and hide, get low, and disappear, but I sat there and watched her speak to me, catching fragments of what she was saying to me. Am I suicidal or homicidal, or do I want an open or closed adoption? Ms. Whoever you are, because I didn't know her name, please get out of my face before I hit you. I'm not going to hurt myself now, so move.

She jumped back and allowed me passage. I had to get home. I felt so unbalanced and out of place. I needed to collect myself and formulate a plan, and I needed to get out of that building. I was suffocating; I needed air. Outside, it seemed like everything was moving in slow motion, and the air felt thick, almost hard to breathe. As I inhaled, it burned my nose and throat. I could feel bile churning in my stomach and threatening to come up and out, but I held it in and made my way home feeling defeated.

I hailed a cab and got in, rolled the window down, told the driver where I was headed, closed my eyes, and just let the wind caress my face and tried to bring calmness to my soul before I got home.

Finally, I made it home, paid the driver, thanked him, and walked into my building. As I got off the elevator, I could hear Sam playing with his beat equipment in the apartment from the hallway. Rolling my eyes, it seems like every time I put my key in the door. Sam was there, and, at that moment, I just needed to be by myself. Why was he there? I put my key in the door, turned the knob, and entered the sight of Sam, set off a series of explosions inside of me, and on this day, I let it all fly. I slammed the door and erupted into a frenzy. Yelling and screaming at him, how could he do this shit to me and on purpose? Yeah, I felt like it was a step up, being that I miscarried his baby the year before, and after that, we used condoms. He was trying to trap me.

What kind of lame-ass Wild African American traps a girl? Is it not supposed to be the other way around? He sat there listening to me as I screamed at the top of my lungs until I was hoarse, and hot salty tears streamed down my face. He simply looked up at me with this stupid expression on his face and laughed at me like I was a fucking joke. I leaped from where I stood to the couch and started to attack him. Sam, being bigger and stronger than me, didn't make a difference in the world. I was kicking, crawling, biting, punching, and yelling like a Tasmania devil. Sam finally pinned me down and got me to calm down. He asked me what happened and what was wrong. I struggled a little under his weight so I could look into his eyes and say it's too late; I cannot get rid of this baby.

He seemed relieved and happy, and I was confused as to why he was happy. I didn't know that he felt like this would be his last time to attempt to raise a family. To have one of his children grow up in a two-parent household. The thought was sweet, so I said fuck it and suck it up, butter cup. It is what it is at this point, and this baby is coming one way or another.

CHAPTER 13: PREGNANCY WOES

This wasn't an easy pregnancy for me. I had every symptom that you could imagine. This baby had me sick, not eating, not sleeping, I was losing weight, and I was irritable. Trying to stay out of the hospital was my top priority, and that was no easy feat. It took a lot of tears and promises to eat well and stay hydrated. Thank goodness my provider was sympathetic to my tears. At month six, my mother gave me the antidote to morning sickness: red plums, salt, and Italian salad dressing. I was annoyed that she had withheld this information and hadn't told me sooner. She at least could have saved me from the everyday sickness.

During the rest of my pregnancy, I was completing my nursing program and trying my best to be a loving partner and wife, and for a while, we had found a mutual blissful place of existence. Now, when I told my father I was pregnant, he said that I was going to have a boy and he would be born on his birthday, 12/06, and I scoffed at him and said yeah, right, I don't even know what I'm having. Then came my official sonogram, where they told Sam and me the sex of the baby and the predicted date of birth, which was December 17th. Well, it looks like my dad was partially right; I was having a boy.

I completed the program, and I graduated on 06/06/06 with my ASN in nursing. I would take my NCLEX in November, a few weeks before I would give birth to God's greatest gift, my heartbeat. My father and one of my older cousins, by about eight years, have birthdays right behind each other, and sometimes they would celebrate together. This was the case in 2006, so on the fifth of December, we all went out to celebrate them, and I was wobbling and dropping it like it was hot belly and all. I got home late at night and got in the bed. My back started to hurt. In fact, it was on fire. Later, I would be told I was having back labor. I figured that it was tension, and a hot shower would loosen my back up. So, I got up and headed into the bathroom. I stripped out of my pajamas, entered the shower, and let the hot water beat on my back. I had been bent over for about 2 minutes, and then this PAIN shot from the top of my head to the bottom of my feet, almost making me fall out of the shower. Thank goodness for towel rails, or I would have hit the floor. I screamed for Sam. He came running into the bathroom, and I was panting. He helped me out of the shower and then left me sitting on top of the toilet. I sat there for a while before I realized that Sam had left without me, so I shuffled into the bedroom to get dressed, and another pain hit, this time making me drop to one knee. I felt arms around me and lift me to the bed. Sam had gone to bring the car closer to the house.

He helped me get dressed and then brought me downstairs and helped me into the car. He took me to Pleasantville Hospital Center, and they asked me a few questions, examined me, and said I was only 2 centimeters (about 0.79 in) dilated and sent me home by the time Sam and I reached home and went back upstairs. I told Sam to call 911 because I was in immense pain and needed them to run all the red lights. He did as he was told and called 911. When they got to me, I was about 6 centimeters (about 2.36 in) dilated, and thank you, Jesus. They safely ran all the red lights. When we arrived back at the hospital, the nurses laughed and said you just left. Why are you back so soon? I said because I'm in labor, why the fuck else would I be back here, so they checked me, and low and behold, I'm now 7 centimeters (about 2.76 in). They admitted me and sent Sam and me to labor and delivery. They sent the anesthesiologist to put in my epidural. He said he would not be able to give me the epidural because I was too far dilated, and when I told you, everyone on that floor heard the evil words that came out of my mouth. I frightened the devil himself.

That poor man was shaking, but he damn sure put in the epidural. I actually drifted off to sleep for about an hour. I was awoken by tremendous pressure in my rectum, so I knew it was time to push. I reached over and pressed the call button to alert the nurse that I was ready to push. The nurse came in. She was a little rude and barked how can she could help me. I told her that I was ready to push. She snarked, "How would you know?" Of course, I hadn't told anyone that I was a nurse as well and I know the signs and symptoms. So, it was sad to be treated with such disdain by my fellow nurse. I said, please check me. I knew I was fully dilated, not wanting to let my normal angry bitch out because I needed their help. The nasty nurse asked me to spread my legs, checked my cervix, and said, "Well, wouldn't you know it? You are fully dilated!"

I wanted to say, "No shit, Sherlock," but I just smiled and nodded. Sam stroked my hand and smiled at me, and with this boyish look on his face, said, "He is coming, Monie, he's coming." At that very moment, I felt like my life was exiting my body, so I asked for help. The nurses gave me this lame excuse of how women have been having babies since the Stone Age, and I would be all alright. I was just nervous, but I knew something was off, so I unhooked myself from the monitors and tried to walk to the hallway. Sam asked me what I was doing, and I told him to get help. The very next thing I can remember is waking up with my father and Sam on either side of me. My father, looking down at me, said, "Good job, BooBoo. You did such a good job." At the foot of my bed was a nurse, and she asked me if I wanted to see my son. I managed to say no before I passed back out. I had been rushed into emergency surgery and given a C-section. Apparently, I had been hemorrhaging, and the baby had ingested the blood and gone into fetal distress. Seems like he and I were bonded not only by genetics but by a near-death experience.

The next morning, 12/07/2006, I woke up, thanked God to be here, and dragged myself to the baby neonatal intensive care unit. I asked to see baby boy Mitchell Crawford, and the nurse pushed a small white baby in an incubator to me, and instantly, I was outraged. Why would this nurse be playing with me and bring me a white woman's baby? Why would she do that when I'm clearly a woman of color? So, I laughed and said no, miss, this is not my baby. She looked at the tag on the incubator and said yes, momma, this is your baby, so I called Sam and asked what does the baby look like. He answered and said a baby? Like, what are you talking about? Enraged, I yelled no, dummy, what the hell does he look like and he said white with dark hair. and I felt silly. I had forgotten that black women carry the EVE gene, so we could have any color baby at any time. So, this is why mine was white for the time being, at least. So, I looked into his small little face, and for the very first time, I fell in actual love for when I looked at him, I instantly melted. He had me, and he didn't even have to speak. He was simply my heart living outside of my chest and I had never known a love like this, and this love I would protect at all costs.

CHAPTER 14: BABY BLUES

The next morning, December 7th, 2006, I woke up, thanked God to be here, and dragged myself to the baby's neonatal intensive care unit. I asked to see baby boy Mitchell Crawford, and the nurse pushed a small white baby in an incubator to me, and instantly, I was outraged. Why would this nurse be playing with me and bringing me a white woman's baby? Why would she do that when I'm clearly a woman of color? So, I laughed and said no, miss, this is not my baby. She looked at the tag on the incubator and said, "Yes, momma, this is your baby." So, I called Sam and asked him, "Hey, what does the baby look like?" He answered and said a baby? Like, what are you talking about? I yelled, "No, dummy, what the hell does he look like." He said white with dark hair, and I felt silly. I had forgotten that black women carry the EVE gene so that we could have any color baby at any time. So, this is why mine was white for the time being, at least. So, I looked into his small little face, and at that very instance, I fell in actual love when an overwhelming emotion surged through my body, and I instantly melted. He had me, and he didn't even have to speak. He was simply my heart living outside of my chest and I had never known a love like this, and this love I would protect at all costs.

You would think motherhood would be easy after I said all of that. However, I suffered from post-partum depression and would only pick him up to breastfeed him, change him, or clean him. Luckily for me, Legend was an excellent baby. He slept through the night and barely cried. I thought something was wrong with him. So, of course, I brought him to the pediatrician with all my new mom craziness and told him that I felt like I was failing him. However, he assured me that Legend was healthy and to simply allow him to adjust to his new environment at his own rate if he is asleep, I should be asleep too. Since having Legend, things with his father, my husband, and soon-to-be ex-husband were ok. We smoothed most of our issues out, and things at home were peaceful. Unfortunately, the depression that I was in killed my sex drive and made me mean, rude, and cold toward Sam. Honestly, I was just a horrible person to him, and it didn't make it better that his way of showing love was to annoy and torture me with his childish ways. So, at the very least, the peaceful short-term house soon became a war zone again. Every time he would enter the house, I would ask why are you here? Every time I asked for money, it was, why are you tricking on someone? So, I needed to get out of that house, away from Sam and away from Legend. I didn't want my negative energy to affect my baby. I needed an outlet. I needed a way out of the pressures of dealing with a man I could no longer tolerate and a baby that I loved with all my heart but was scared to revisit all of my childhood trauma. I was so scared that I would become my parents I forgot to be a parent and a wife. I failed at my marriage and let it fall to pieces. I didn't take pride in the fact that I had a husband. To me, it was solely in name. He was back to cheating openly, and I acted as if it didn't bother me. When, in fact, this time around, it crushed me. I just didn't have the means to express that to Sam or to let him know that I actually wanted things to work. Unfortunately, I didn't know how to be a wife, nor did I even try.

Once my depression partially lifted and I was able to focus on something other than my failed marriage and trying not to scar my infant son, I reached out to my pharmacology professor and told him I needed help obtaining a job. Professor Eng was now an ADN at Bronco Medical Center in the Bluff. He told me to come in on a Tuesday around 2:30 p.m. I agreed to the day and time. I reached out to my mother and begged her to watch Legend for me. Of course, that came with a cost, so now I had to beg Sam for cash so that my mother could watch Legend whilst I went to this interview. Once I dropped the baby off at my mother's, I headed up to the Bluff. Professor Eng was standing in the lobby when I arrived. He was about 5'11 portly with dark brown eyes and a goofy, nerdy look to himself. Eng brought me upstairs to the infamous Cloud 8 and presented me to the then-nurse manager, Rebecca Smith. He told her she was to hire me, and he walked out of her office, leaving me standing in front of this stranger who would become my first boss as a registered nurse. My hire date at Bronco was July 7th, 2007, and I have been with them ever since.

I have done some per diem work at other hospitals, but Bronco has been my bread and butter. To date, I have worked on a medical-surgical unit (med-surg), an outpatient oncology clinic, and as a nurse navigator all within Bronco. Bronco has become a second home to me shit. I spend more hours there than anywhere else, and I have developed some amazing connections and gotten into trouble more than I would like (those damn ADNs), but I continue to strive for my own personal excellence and my own personal goals, and when I reach a goal, I make sure there is a new one to achieve. As far back as I can remember, I have been Nurse Monique even before officially becoming Nurse Monique. I have had the need to make sure that everyone is good or well taken care of before even thinking of myself. The pleasure I get from helping someone in need is immeasurable. Being able to be a part of something so much bigger than myself fills me with pride. I was told from an early age to be a nurse. I was compassionate, selfless, and caring. However, I feel that nursing is so much more than that. To me, nursing is being stern yet gentle when patients refuse treatment or care. My nursing is having thick skin when patients call you stupid for the 100th time in a day. My nursing is being a listening ear and a shoulder to lean on. I'm relatable because I have lived a hard life and come out on the other side beat up scarred yet standing taller than ever. My nursing comes from the purest part of my heart because, honestly, if your heart ain't in this, it will drain and burn you out.So here I am, still doing what I've been called to do. Saving lives.

Chapter 15: Everything is Dysfunctional

You would think that at this point in my life, I would be more put together. However, I have to let y'all know I was suffering from chronic depression and post-partum, still trying to hold my family down and still being a parent to my parents. Whenever something went wrong, one or both of my parents would call me. My father struggling with his addictions, and my mother struggling with letting men rule over her and her household. Unfortunately, I have not found my voice yet, nor have I learned how to prioritize myself first. So, for lack of better words, I was the flunky of the family. Run here, get me this. I need to find a rehab. I'm having surgery, and someone needs to watch the kids. I'm burning on both sides of this candle, and I don't know how much light I had left to give the world, but I need to figure something out because everything in my life is suffering or coming to an end. This was taking a toll on me mentally, physically, and emotionally. I was on the verge of a mental and physical breakdown, down and the first thing to completely unravel before I was able to contain myself was that ill-fated marriage I was in.

Sam and I had been living a dysfunctional life for way too long now, and I could no longer tow the lines of trying to keep a man I no longer loved happy and keeping my sanity. Sam had come home late one night after spending the day with one of his women, and I started an argument, "Why do you keep coming back here when you're clearly happier with anyone besides me?" It was an honest question that I guess offended him and he flipped out and told me to get out. And stupid me, with my name on the lease and paying half the bills, I asked for him to give me a month to find housing for Legend and myself. However, Sam is an asshole and said he'd give me a week.

His wife, the mother of his only son! Give me a week! Ok cool! I told him I'd be out by tomorrow, and the only thing I asked was he hold Legend down until I found a place to stay, which took me about three months, but on my weekends off and every off day, no matter how tired I was I went and got my baby. Sam was really a nasty piece of work. He did everything in his power to make life difficult for me, and he did so all while dating another woman. Still married to me. My name was on the lease, yet he moved her right in the day after I moved out. How much love and devotion did he have for his family? None, if you ask me. However, he told anyone who would listen that it was all me and that I have always been a horrible, manipulative person, and he was glad to be ending this marriage. But hey, no matter what the truth is, that relationship had run its course a long time ago, and I had stayed longer than I should have because I was trying to give Legend something I had never had.

I truly wanted him to grow up in a two-parent household, but my sanity and sense of peace also needed to be taken care of, and staying with Sam, one of us, wasn't going to make it. Once I found a place close to my job, I applied, and within three weeks, I was moved in. I went and got Legend, and we slept on an air mattress until my furniture arrived a month later, but that was no big thing. Legend is my heart in human form, and I loved the closeness we shared. Legend has been the best gift I have ever received. That child is my light in the darkness. My hopes and dreams balled into one person the absolute best parts of me walking outside of me. I'm so blessed to have him as my son and my rider. Inside joke "Cause I Don't Fucking Play About My Mother!"

Chapter 16: Dating Again

A year after I separated from Sam, I started dating, and let me tell you, there are a lot of rejects in that dating pool. I met this one guy named Reginald, who was a train operator for the MTA, on a dating app called Plenty of Leaves. Anyway, we never spoke verbally, and after I think about it, he more than likely had Tourette syndrome. We only texted, and we decided to meet up and go out to eat now. I had been working the night shift, so my mother had given me a care package that included a pocket knife, a taser, and a flashlight for my safety. I carried the taser more often than I did the knife or flashlight, so of course, during this meeting with a complete stranger that I met on a dating app, I brought my taser and had it in my coat pocket. So, Reginald picks me up; he is standing by the passenger door of his 2010 Acura. He opens my door and helps me in. Wow, what a gentleman, I'm thinking to myself. So, I'm seated, and I lean over and open the door. I show that in a movie, and I thought that's the way to show a guy you like him, so a small and simple gesture can go a long way. He gets in, thanks me for opening his door, puts his seatbelt on, and starts the car. As we pull off and approach the light, he bangs on the steering wheel and yells FUCK! I jumped and said, "Yo, bro, you alright?" Reginald assures me he's ok and continues to drive. We are both sitting in silence, but my hand is now in my pocket on the taser. When he does it again bangs on the steering wheel and yells FUCK! I again jump and now say look, we can reschedule because now I'm panicking, looking over my shoulder to see if someone was in the back seat cause they were plotting to kidnap me. Reginald started speaking, telling me how much he was looking forward to taking me out and that he didn't want to reschedule when his arm flung across my chest. He yells FUCK, and almost simultaneously, my hand comes out of my pocket, and I tase him in the neck. I jumped out of his moving car, ran up a block, and down two more blocks. I never looked back to see if he was okay or even following me. I finally stopped running because I was out of breath. The flight-or-fight instinct is a real thing cause y'all when I tell y'all I took flight, I took flight! Needless to say, I have never heard from Reginald again, nor have I ever gone back on Plenty of Leaves.

Now, you know, after that, I got off dating sites for a while and was not even thinking about dating. Somehow, I ran into someone at work. She… yes, she! She was coming to visit her mother, who just so happened to be my patient, and she would always come after five, so I thought she was coming after work. To my surprise, she didn't work. She did, however, take care of her mother, but this was before you could become a family member's home health aide, so she had no job, and yeah, it was my fault for assuming she worked. However, I've never been the type of person to worry about what's in your pocket because I can hold my own. I've always been independent, so it wasn't a big deal at first. Spending money on her, taking her out, and moving her in was fun for a while, but instead of a partner, I had an extra-broke roommate who I would have sex with from time to time. And as time went on, I started to become irritated; however, I didn't express it because I didn't want to hurt her feelings. It was my fault. I should have let her know what I was feeling and thought maybe things would have ended differently. Anyway, I was so nice even after we broke up.

I was allowing her to stay rent-free until she finished school. And everyone thought I was crazy, but I still cared for her and wanted her to do well. Until one night, I wanted to have some company and asked if she could go over to her friend's house, who lives in the same complex as I do. She misheard what I had said and, in return, said some horrible shit to me. So I let all of my pent-up frustration and aggravation out in a verbal assault, and that was it. She had to get out. That blow-up was the catalyst to the very end of any kind of relationship we might have had or continued. The soft and caring

Monique was gone, and I wanted and needed her out of my house before I did something stupid and I would regret it.

Now that I kicked her out and she gave me my keys, you would think that would be the end of it, but oh no, shortly two weeks later, she showed up with the police to make me let her back in because she had squatters and roommate rights. Now, at the time, I didn't know that once she gave me back my keys, she self-terminated those rights. So I had to let her back in and, in doing so, put on my petty Betty face and took all the sheets and towels, toilet paper, and disposable wipes out of the linen closet. She thought she was getting back in my bed. No, ma'am, you sleep on the couch in your clothes. I'm to provide a place to sleep and nothing else. When I get up to leave, it is time for you to go. Do not open my refrigerator or cabinets. Ain't nothing in here for you but the couch, sink, toilet, and shower, and you must provide your own toiletries. Eventually, she left because of how I treated her, but can you blame me? I had been nothing but nice to her since the breakup and asked for one simple thing, and she went ham on me. The nerve of her. When I was damn near the only person looking out for her, but I digress. I had to go to court and mail her a thirty-day notice of intent to evict. When she finally received her notice, she came back with her brother, whom I also had been holding some of his stuff when they had been evicted from their mother's home. And they got all their stuff and finally moved out. Maybe about two years later, she would stop by to apologize and explain what happened from her side. I listened, fed her, and told her I understood and there was no bad blood and I wished her well.

Oh, but the dating stories get worse; however, this is the last one, and then I'll move on to a funny story. After dating this lady whom I met in the hospital, I said no more dating apps and no more hospitals. Now, the problem is people don't stop me and ask me out to buy me drinks. The fact of the matter is every relationship I have been in has been someone setting me up with a friend or cousin, so dating for me has never been easy. If I'm approached, they're already involved, married, or in a complicated situation. With that being said, I fell back into dating sites. This one was called Blender, and I chatted with a few people; however, one guy was a little more persistent than the others, so I started to focus on him. He worked for a hospital, too, but it's in Canton. I made sure to speak to him on the phone because I didn't want a repeat of the Tourette guy. He had a nice voice, so we chatted for about a month before he actually worked up the courage to ask if he could bring me lunch at my job. He lived about fifteen minutes from my job, so I said yes. He actually cooked for me and brought me salmon, rice, and veggies, and it was alright; there was nothing to brag about. Still, I was thankful since I hadn't cooked the night before. We sat in one of the conference rooms before he had to head off to work, and I felt a little hopeful about this one who I'll call Gunnar. Gunnar had been morbidly obese and lost about three hundred fifty pounds, and he was still a little chunky in his torso area, but he had a nice smile, and he seemed nice enough. So, we continued to talk on the phone, we went out a few times, and then, finally, I spent the night over. Can we say the top five of worst sex ever? Gunnar has a baby penis. No, I really mean it was the size of my thumb fully erect, and on top of that, he had erectile dysfunction from his diabetes. Now, here's the joke: he asked me to deep-throat it. I couldn't help but laugh and ask, "Deep throat, what?" I was really confused as to what he was asking me to do. He repeated himself, and I said, "Yeah, I don't have deep-throating skills," so I wouldn't hurt his feelings. Right, I'm always sacrificing myself for everyone else's feelings. Anyway, I would try to make things work; however, deep in my soul, I knew I'd end up cheating on him. And no, sex isn't everything. However, it means a whole lot to be in a relationship and not sexually fulfilled. So, I started doing little things that I knew would annoy him. This would snowball and lead to us getting into a huge fight, with him coming to my job and us breaking up at my job. Now, I don't play about my coins, so it definitely was an automatic termination. I know I said funny story, right? Well, here's the kicker. After I broke up this eight-week relationship, he had his mama call me and try to psychoanalyze me and help us get back together because her son, you know, the one with the little ding a ling loved me. Which grown man has his mama call someone not once but twice to try and convince me that I was making a huge mistake and needed to take her son back? After he stalked me for about two weeks, popping up around my complex with this hideous bright orange coat. Yeah, that's a no. I hear that he met a lovely lady and is doing well. Stalker vibes and momma boys are red flags if I ever saw one. The moral of these dating stories is that you shouldn't settle for just anyone who smiles on your face. I'm no longer willing to settle for bull shit in my love life, social life, work life, or with anything that comes close enough to my orbit. I'm finally learning to free myself from the confines and restraints of everyone's feelings. One last development on the dating front: I'm extremely happy with the man in my life right now. I've mentioned him and already said we've come full circle. I just wanted to thank him for sticking by me through thick and thin sickness and in health, and we ain't even married. Thank you, Amare, for bringing my glow back. We are Just getting started.

CHAPTER 17: FAMILY

I have had many adventures in this life of mine; however, the most special ones are the ones I have shared with Legend. Boy, have we done everything from mother and son dates to vacations, matching tattoos to even being admitted to the hospital at the same time? We are a dynamic duo. My heart is outside of my body. And this is the last memory I'll leave y'all with. One of my coworkers gave me weed-infused banana bread as a Christmas gift. And before you ask, yes, I knew it had the weed in it. So I get home, take my shower, and hop in my bed. Mind you, this is my first experience with edibles of any kind, so I take a little sliver of the banana bread and start watching TV. I realize that I feel nothing and nothing fun or funny has happened, so my dumb ass eats half of the loaf.

Now, I'm not sure when Legend walked into my room, but I do know we started talking, and he asked me if I was high. I remember saying I think so, and he then replied go to bed.

Now, I'm not sure when he left the room, but I do know that my bed was trying to swallow me. I was drowning and couldn't get out of bed. Now, I was screaming at the top of my lungs for Legend's help, but to no avail. He never came to my rescue, so I succumbed to the pull of my bed, said a prayer, and told Legend I loved him. When I woke up in the morning, I was pissed. I stormed into Legends room ranting and raving, and he looked up at me as confused as a tick on a melon.

"How could you not come to check in on me? I was screaming for you for like ten minutes. I could have died, and then what?" He started to laugh at me and said, "Ma, come on, if you were screaming like that, do you really think I wouldn't have come to see what was going on." he said before he left my room. I rolled over on my side and was knocked out. So now I'm standing in his room looking like a damn asshole, not sure if I should believe him or not, so I settled with real son, no apology, nothing. The only thing I said is, do you want some breakfast? Now, every night between the hours of 9 pm and 10:30 pm, he comes into my room, says good night, turns off my television and lights, walks out and closes the door. When did I become the child in this situation? Truth be told, I wouldn't have it any other way. That child is the true love of my life, and, no, I wouldn't die for him but live for him to keep him safe and secure as long as I possibly can. I'm truly proud of the young man. He is seventeen and soon leaving the nest. Smart, independent, handsome, and lives life the way that he sees fit. He is self-fulfilled and doesn't need anyone's approval or acknowledgement to make him feel worthy of love because he knows that he is worth that and more.

Now all my siblings are grown, even Riley. She's 20. Joy has four kids and one grandchild, Kevin Jr. has three girls, Gabby has one of each, Jet has a daughter, and Jim and Riley have none so far. We are a magically blended bunch of unicorns. We fight, make up, laugh, celebrate, and cry together. Are we as close as we were as children? No, but the love is always there. Gabby has separated herself from most of her siblings, but she keeps in touch with Legend, Riley, and Kevin, so there is hope there. I try to keep the gaps between us as small as possible. It truly doesn't matter that I'm the main connecting factor. The fact is that we are one, and we all rock for one another. Along the way, I've adopted three more siblings: Kevin Jr and Gabby have a younger brother and sisters, Tonya, Greg and Cami. For a long time, we thought Cami was my father's daughter. However, ancestry helped us solve that mystery. So now we are just one deranged group of individuals that have many flaws, but the love we all share isn't one of them. Love is simple and in its purest form. We may not all share the same lineage, but that doesn't matter. The binding agent is me, and hopefully, one day, we all will sit down, laugh as one collective, and talk about how our parents sucked at being parents, and we still prevailed and made something out of ourselves.

POSTFACE

Through the mental, emotional, and physical abuse, I have become stronger, wiser, and risen to every occasion. I have tried to be a guiding light and an armored shield. I guess you could say I'm a first responder for my family, lol. I can say I'm proud to be the first person on either side of my immediate family with any kind of college degree or career. I'm the first to push myself beyond what I was told I could be. I was the first to want more and achieve more. The keyword here is the first. Since I paved the way and showed my family that we don't have to settle for welfare checks or government aid, I gladly passed the baton, and they have leveled up themselves, and I could not be prouder of my family. We've come from struggles, from drugs, from poverty, from pain, and chaos; however, we have excelled, shined, and given the naysayers something to talk about. There is a greatness in my family long ago beaten out of and buried with our ancestors. This greatness is being revived within me and those who have and will follow in my footsteps. I can't see the future; however, I know it is bright and glorious.

I say all this because what I ultimately learned is that your biggest obstacle in life is yourself. Nothing else can stand in your way, not the sun, not the rain, not your friends, not your family, no one. Yeah, it is nice to have a cheering squad in your section. However, we must learn to be our own cheering squad because sometimes those rafters are quiet and empty. Sometimes, those who should rally behind and next to you are trying to pull you down to depths you cannot escape. And no matter the circumstances, you never stop moving, you never stop believing you crush everything thrown at you, and when you reach the top, turn around and pull someone up with you. When people look at me today, they don't see my struggles, my heartbreaks, and my mistakes that turned into life lessons. They can't see my faith, for I know without God, I would have fallen and not gotten back up. They can only see that I've made it.

No, I wouldn't say that I'm unstoppable. However, I will say I'm unbreakable. When people say they are cut from a different cloth, that could never be me because I'm not made from cloth. Cloth can be ripped, burnt, and torn to pieces. No, I'm solid. I'm made from stone. I cannot fold. I don't know how to fold. Yeah. Unbreakable, I like that better.

Ok, let's start wrapping this up. My name is Monique, and yes, I've been through the windmill and had my share of ups and downs; however, my heart is pure. I love deeply, and should I love you, then you have my trust, and should I happen to trust you, then you have my loyalty, and the only person who can mess that up is yourself. By no means am I perfect, nor do I consider myself to be perfect; however, I'm perfectly flawed and divinely made. I'm God modified and unapologetically me. Simply put, I'm me, and I'm grateful for the life God saw fit for me to have because I'm extremely blessed.

My family and I have come full circle, and the majority of us are Happy and Healthy. Another inside joke. We all have gone through the wringer and struggled with many adversities, but we've made it to the other side, and the skies are brighter and full of possibilities.

When I was younger, I wholeheartedly wanted to be in another family; however, I wouldn't want to be in any other family because when I tell you I have memories upon memories to look back on and keep me laughing and keep me grounded in the present and excited for the future so that we can make many more happy memories. I was raised in the chaos, in drama, and have found an understanding and love for it. I love what my family and I have become, and we have come a long way from homeless, crackheads, BCW\ACS cases, and young parents to being stable, hard, working almost picture perfect. My father told me something the other day that I now hold close to my heart. He said you must enjoy your moments. Live for you and forget about all the other crap that's going on. In the end, "BooBoo is another name I hate." In the end, BooBoo, all that really matters is the period. You know what? He is correct, so I'm enjoying every moment and letting things fall and grow as they should.

Through all the unfortunate events that have plagued my life. I have found solace and comfort in helping those who need healing. I have grown to love a position that I had been forced into. I have just finally accepted that being Nurse Monique is not having to sacrifice myself for the greater good of others and leaving myself on the back burner of the stove in the next apartment. I have learned that I can still be this amazing, loving person who can heal others without neglecting myself. Self-love is important. You can't continue to draw from a well that has not been replenished. Everything needs refueling. I have also found that I needed the most healing, and while drafting this story, I have started my healing process. I have kept my thoughts and feelings bottled up for so long that it has started to manifest itself as illness, so it's time to detox, cleanse, and let go. I need to heal others, but I need to be healthy and healed to continue providing that love and my stellar positive energy that everyone looks to me for. I have spent years of my life looking out the 12th-floor window in the projects, looking for love, happiness, joy, and stability, and I found that instead of looking outward, I should have been looking inward and loving myself the whole time because I'm worthy of self-love.

This book is dedicated to three people who have been instrumental in my life. Pops, Grit, thank y'all for allowing me to fall and get back up by myself. Thank you for the drama you have brought into my life. You guys put me into the exact position that I needed to succeed in this life, and to my son, know that you saved me more than you'll ever know. You are truly the reason why my heart beats, why I breathe the air, and why I pound the streets. You are truly my everything. These three people have helped shape me into the woman that I am today. We may not see eye to eye most of the time. However, my world revolves around y'all. I will stop, drop, and roll to ensure that y'all always feel loved and know that I love you from the deepest part of my soul. I will constantly strive for more because they have taught me that I'm way more than a daughter and a mother. I'm the living, breathing representative of what success looks like in adversity. I thank God for all of you and the roles you all have played in my life. A special thank you to my aunt Sherrae "forever a Michelle thing." you are always in my heart. Thank you for showing me that no matter what the circumstances, I can always come out on top and never stop reinventing myself to be the best version of myself that I can be. Truth be told, I'm grateful for almost every person who has come into my life for a reason, a season, or a lesson. You all have been teachers in my life and inadvertently made me this beautifully strong yet vulnerable woman you see before you.

And a great big Thank you to all of you for coming on this journey with me. And to all those that helped me along the way while I looked out those project windows as my personal therapy session to clear my mind and recenter myself because I have been on and off this damn merry-go-round for years. I can finally say I love myself. I'm putting myself first, and it never felt so damn good! ☺ My therapist would be so proud of me!